"FIRE!"

I leaped up and yanked up the shade. Smoke boiled over the trees and I could hear the cows bellowing. They were trapped inside the fences. I ran downstairs and grabbed Rider out of his crib. Jonah was sitting on the couch trembling, clutching his blanket to his chest. I thrust Rider at him. "Watch him," I said. "I'll help Grandpa get the cows out of the field."

"Rachel!" Grandpa shouted. "Drive them into the garden."

I chased after the cows, driving them toward the garden gate. Then I pushed the gate closed behind them and turned back toward the house. I couldn't see flames from where I was so the fire was going out.

I opened the back door and shouted for Jonah. No answer.

"Rider? Jonah? Don't hide from me now. It's not funny!" The house was empty. I found Jonah hiding under the back porch. His eyes were swollen from crying.

I swallowed. "Where's Rider?" I asked, my voice shaking.

"Gone," Jonah wept. He hid his face. "Gone."

RACHEL CHANCE

JEAN THESMAN

AN AVON  FLARE BOOK

AVON BOOKS
A division of
The Hearst Corporation
1350 Avenue of the Americas
New York, New York 10019

Copyright © 1990 by Jean Thesman
Published by arrangement with Houghton Mifflin Company
Library of Congress Catalog Card Number: 89-28582
ISBN: 0-380-71378-0
RL: 5.1

First Avon Flare Printing: November 1992

AVON FLARE TRADEMARK REG. U.S. PAT. OFF. AND IN OTHER COUNTRIES, MARCA REGISTRADA, HECHO EN U.S.A.

Printed in the U.S.A.

RA 10 9 8 7 6 5 4 3 2 1

Once more, for my family.

RACHEL CHANCE

One

My name is Rachel Chance, and I turned fifteen in July 1940, four weeks after my brother was stolen.

That terrible summer dulled Mama's fair, curling hair and humbled my proud grandfather. And it silenced Cousin Jonah's singing. Time stopped, and each day turned back on itself like a weary old dog chasing his tail. Rider was gone.

I learned what children should never know, that adults are helpless, too, and sometimes even honorable people lie and steal and whisper plans in the dark.

I remember my birthday that year, when I sat before my cake with its lighted candles and wished not just that we could have Rider back, but that I would live to see the suffering of the ones who stole him.

"Blow out the candles," demanded Henry Webster, the sixteen-year-old boy Grandpa hired to help with the heavy chores. He was a guest at our table by Grandpa's invitation, not mine, for Hank and I cordially despised one another and on his own he would have no more attended my birthday dinner than he would have admitted that I could throw rocks farther and more accurately than he.

"I'll blow them out when I'm ready," I said, scowling.

"Oh, Rachel," Mama said, with a faint sigh.

"Blow!" shouted Grandpa. He was not much taller than Mama, but his voice rattled windows.

I blew and all the candles went out. No one smiled.

"What did you wish?" Hank asked.

"It won't come true if I tell," I said. I had a vision of doom and destruction dancing in my imagination, but even if I had wanted to risk spoiling it by sharing its delightful horrors, the sight of Mama's face guaranteed my silence.

In those awful days, we seldom made it through a meal without her losing interest in her food and turning her attention inward, sometimes even whispering to herself while the rest of us finished eating in uncomfortable silence. Mama, according to Grandpa's friend, Druid Annie, was suffering from melancholia. And small wonder, for where was Rider? What was happening to him?

After I cut and served the cake, I opened my gifts. Mama gave me a new blouse, and Grandpa presented me with a pocketknife with a horn handle. Hank gave me a dollar bill, a fortune in those times, in a homemade birthday card. And Jonah, who may or may not have understood the idea of birthdays, gave me the ball he and Rider had played with before Rider was stolen away from our yard.

That ended the party. As soon as Mama saw the ball, she burst out crying and left the table. Jonah, thirteen but with a mind like a five-year-old, began howling until Banjo,

2

our dog, howled, too, and Grandpa dragged both of them outside.

"Goldang it!" he cried. "It's getting so that a man can't sit down at the table anymore without hooting and hollering starting up and souring the dingbusted milk!" He didn't scare anyone — we all knew that was how he hid his pain.

The door slammed behind him. In the silence, Hank looked at me and I looked steadfastly at him. I wasn't embarrassed, since his family was even more bizarre than mine. While we Chances were only artless and eccentric, the Websters ran to mean drunks and jailbirds, with a few missionaries thrown in to confuse everyone.

"Well," Hank said, "happy birthday anyway. It could have been worse."

"How?" I asked.

"Druid Annie could have come," he said.

Grandpa's lady friend was our usual holiday guest and could be counted on to challenge any breach in manners she detected on his part. Their quarrels were formidable, so I gave silent thanks to the emergency that had called Druid Annie away before we sat down to dinner. The evening had been nerve-racking enough.

Hank went home, Jonah and Banjo wandered back inside at nightfall, and Mama appeared, wraithlike, to help with the dishes. My birthday was over. I went to bed and stared into the dark.

*

This is how we came to have Rider and then lose him.

After my father, William Chance, died in 1933, we moved in with my grandfather, Abel Chance, at Rider's

3

Dock, a small town north of Seattle. Mama's parents, the Riders of Rider's Dock, had died years before; she had no other blood relatives, and so it was natural that she would make the large but scattered Chance family her own.

I don't remember the day we moved to Grandpa's farm, but he assured me often that it was a day not soon forgotten by anyone else.

"You screamed for three straight hours," he'd say, "and Jonah finally sang you to sleep." Jonah, a cousin I barely knew, would have frightened any other eight-year-old child, but I had been saturated with misery by the other events, so poor Jonah, retarded and disfigured, must have seemed unremarkable. In fact, my bellowing probably frightened him.

"You made so much racket that the cow dried up and the chickens quit laying," Grandpa would go on, when he recalled those first days on the farm. "I wasn't sure if you were my own son's girl or a surprise left behind by some stranger. I should have sneaked you over to Druid Annie to see if she could have done something about you. At least, the noisemaking part of you."

At this point in Grandpa's recollecting, my mother, Lara, would always laugh, and Jonah, probably not understanding, would laugh, too, and I would scowl, pretending to be angry but actually loving the attention.

Of course, Grandpa's story had to be altered after my brother was born years later, because Rider truly was a stranger's child and Mama would never name his father. After we had Rider, Grandpa would say that he'd really suspected during my first days there that I was a throwback to his Indian great-grandfather whose name (and I swear this is true) was Howling Coyote.

Mama worked to add to Grandpa's small disability pension. He had been injured in the railroad accident that killed his brother, who was Jonah's father. The larger of the town's two churches hired Mama as a secretary, and she received a few dollars and first pick of the clothes donated to the poor by the town's wealthy citizens, those same people who once had craved the friendship of Mama's parents.

All of us wore the secondhand clothes except Grandpa, who shouted, "I'll go buck naked first, and be damned to them!"

I secretly applauded Grandpa's stand, for the hand-me-downs humiliated me, but I was practical. This was, no doubt, the place where Howling Coyote and I parted company, for we Chances were supposed to inherit pride as a birthright.

When I was nearly thirteen, Rider was born, and he was two weeks old before Mama brought him home from the hospital and put him in my arms.

"Rider Chance, this is your sister," she said, smiling over him.

The baby looked up at me. The moment I saw his shining light gray eyes and black lashes, I knew who his father was.

Rider was born in June. Mama had spent the September before in Spokane, caring for Cousin Samantha Chance Devereaux, who had fallen downstairs and broken her hip.

After she had been gone for three weeks, I began waking early in those sweet, autumn mornings, waiting for her.

We didn't know exactly when she would come, for her letters had become vague and oddly fanciful, reminding me uncomfortably of the older girls in the three-room school where I spent my days. But in my bones I was sure she would return during the last week of September. Morning after morning I lay awake, restless because it was too early to get up and dress for school and too late to fall back to sleep.

Then one calm, quiet morning I heard a car ease up in front of the house and stop in the dirt driveway under my window. I hopped out of bed and ran to look.

A tall man was helping Mama out of a dusty car, and while she waited, whispering to him, he lifted her two suitcases from the back seat and set them on the bottom porch step. Then, to my amazement, Mama raised her face to him and slipped her arms around his neck. He bent his head and kissed her.

Downstairs, Banjo barked sharply. Mama immediately stepped away from the man and, laughing, picked up her suitcases and ran up the porch steps. The man waited until she went inside, and Banjo stopped barking and began squealing instead.

Then the man glanced up, as if he had known all along I was watching. He swept his hat off and bowed to me, with the morning sun shining on his blond hair. When he looked up again I saw that he had remarkable, clear gray eyes shadowed by long, dark lashes, and I wasn't certain, for a moment, that he was real. I half expected him to disappear in a flash of bright light.

"So you are the black-eyed, black-haired daughter," he

said. "Do you love yourself, Rachel? Even half as much as I've loved hearing your mother speak of you?"

I nodded dumbly and pressed my hands against my chest. Who was he? Would he stay? I'd never known anyone like him.

"I have other places to go," he said, answering my thought. He bowed to me again. I grinned shakily at him, and he got back into his car and drove away, down the narrow blacktop road that led past Druid Annie's place.

So the next summer, when I looked into my new brother's face and saw those wonderful eyes, I was thrilled, not ashamed. And Grandpa, Jonah, and I set about raising Rider, while Mama looked for work in Rider's Dock. She'd been fired from her church job as soon as the pastor found out she was pregnant.

The grimy little five-and-dime store in downtown Rider's Dock ("downtown" was two blocks wide, three blocks long) hired Mama as a clerk when Rider was five months old. She earned forty cents an hour, and these riches provided us with a wonderful Christmas. Rider, sitting upright on a blanket in the middle of the living room floor, watched us decorate his first tree.

Blond and gently rounded, he had grown to be so beautiful that people stopped us on the street when we had him with us to tell us so. And this made all of us happy, even when they added, "Too bad he's illegitimate."

Jonah, who didn't know what "illegitimate" meant (and just as well, since he and Rider had that much in common), would always nod his poor, misshapen head and cry, "Yes! Yes!" until those who had spoken to us hurried away, fear-

7

ful that their comments about Rider might be taken as an offer to become involved in our family's tangled affairs.

The pastor at the church, eventually hearing that Mama had found work, came to see her one Saturday morning in January and missed her by five minutes. Unfortunately we'd had no premonition of his visit, so he caught us at a vulnerable moment.

Grandpa always shaved on the porch, summer and winter. Each morning he carried a pan of hot water out to the porch, set it on the broad rail, and limped back to the kitchen, to gather up his safety razor, soap, and towel. A foggy old mirror, round, with a tin back, hung permanently on one of the porch posts, entangled in the silver lace vine, which was bare and ugly in winter.

On that particular morning, Grandpa was halfway through his shave when Rider, Jonah, and I, all bundled up against the cold, joined him. Below us on the ground, the chickens scratched halfheartedly, their feathers fluffed up. Banjo napped, his head resting near Grandpa's booted feet.

"Goddam water's cold before I get through," Grandpa grumbled.

"Why don't you shave in the kitchen or the bathroom?" I asked. "Or why don't you stop shaving and grow a beard?"

"Beard," echoed Jonah, who'd begun unraveling his old knitted scarf and winding the yarn into a ball. I should have stopped him, but I didn't.

"I could grow a fine beard," Grandpa said, screwing his face to one side and scraping at his skin. We all screwed our faces to one side, even Rider. "Yessir, I might just do

8

it. I could let it grow until the Depression's over. Or maybe until somebody shoots that Hitler over there in Germany."

"Why?" I asked.

Grandpa cocked his head to study his neck in the mirror. "Because he's mean and crazy."

"Crazy," Jonah said. Jonah had no ears, but he could hear just fine through the little holes on the sides of his head. We always put a cap on him when we took him to town, hoping that people wouldn't stare so much. But at home, even in cold weather, we left him alone. Jonah hated caps. Rider, sitting next to him on the glider, looked at him and fingered his own ears curiously.

"Ba," Rider said to Jonah.

"No, crazy," Jonah corrected serenely as he wound yarn.

"Aw, Judas Priest," Grandpa said, touching the towel gingerly to a thin line of blood on his chin. "If I have to listen to their loony conversations much longer, I'm likely to cut my throat just to put an end to my misery. The two of them together are enough to drive a man out of his own wits."

His complaints did not shock or worry me, for I knew him to be a fraud. He loved the boys fiercely and loyally, the way all the Chances loved. "What would you do without them, Grandpa?" I asked, laughing.

It was right then that Pastor Woodie drove around the corner of our house and scattered the squawking chickens in every direction.

"Well, if it ain't God Almighty himself," Grandpa announced as he toweled his face and neck. "Come to strike me dead, have you?" he called out to the tall, fat man struggling out of his car.

"God will settle up with you in his own good time, Abel," Pastor Woodie said. He stared long and hard at nervous Jonah, who had pulled Rider to his lap for safekeeping.

"Look at that," Pastor Woodie said. "Two bastards in one house. Some people in town say that this place isn't a proper home for a young girl. Or for that baby, either."

Grandpa, silent, wiped his razor on his towel.

"Where's your daughter-in-law?" Pastor Woodie asked suddenly. "I want to have a word with her."

"She's gone to work," I said, supplying the answer because Grandpa was not going to say another word.

The chickens wandered back, one by one. Pastor Woodie eyed them for a long moment, scratched his nose thoughtfully, then straightened his hat, ready to get down to business. "I told Lara she could come back to work at the church but she refused."

We all knew why. Since Grandpa was still elaborately ignoring Pastor Woodie, I responded. "That's because you told her she had to give Rider away before she could go back to work for you. She's not going to give Rider away. He's ours!"

Jonah tightened his grip on Rider and echoed, "Ours!"

"She shouldn't be working in that dime store, around all those men who come in to that soda fountain for their lunches. I know what that place is like, Abel. They've got a colored fella in there to play sheet music on the piano. You want your son's widow mixed up with a nigger?"

Grandpa, smiling the smile that the rest of us wisely feared, picked up the pan of cool, soap-scummed water and tipped it over the railing onto Pastor Woodie's trousers and shoes. Pastor Woodie leaped back with a shout, the chickens squawked and flapped, and Jonah laughed wildly. Banjo decided that the interesting events taking place demanded his attention, so he rose to his feet and lunged, snarling and slobbering, at Pastor Woodie, who kicked him until he yelped.

"You old shit!" cried Jonah, completely articulate for once, and he threw the ball of yarn, which was unfortunately connected to his scarf.

The yarn hit Pastor Woodie and bounced into the mud. When Jonah realized that he was still attached to the yarn, he screamed in terror, Rider joined him, and Grandpa roared curses. Pastor Woodie had his car door open but was blocked from escaping by two hysterical hens who had flown inside the car and now flapped dementedly back and forth in the front seat, crapping on everything.

I began to laugh, doubled over, with my legs crossed for fear I would wet my pants. After a moment, Jonah's screams turned to laughter, Rider stopped bawling, and Banjo took refuge under the porch with half a dozen crazy hens. Pastor Woodie opened his other car door and let out the two hens who had thought they were trapped inside — it doesn't take much for a hen to draw the wrong conclusion — and drove away sitting in all that hen mess. Even Grandpa laughed then.

"I wish we'd had time to put the cow in the car," he shouted.

I was helping Jonah untangle himself from the half-unknitted scarf, still laughing, happy at having vanquished one of the Chance family's worst enemies, when a quick chill shook me to my bones and my stomach filled with a poisonous gush of terror. At that instant, Rider looked up at me and I realized I loved him so much that fortune could hold him hostage and break my heart.

❧ Two

My brother, Rider, was stolen in June of 1940, a few days after his second birthday. Before that, my life progressed in typical Chance buck-and-run fashion. Nothing the least bit interesting would happen for months, and then our cautiously arranged affairs would collapse, usually in public. Often, the blame for these disasters could be laid at Grandpa's feet.

For instance, every day except Sunday Grandpa drove to the post office to pick up our mail. He parked his old black pickup truck in front of the Rider's Dock Municipal Building, a two-story, tan wood structure occupied by the mayor, Rider's Dock's three policemen, and Dizzy Snope, the city clerk. The post office was across the street, in the back of Patterson's General Store, and the only people who parked in front of Patterson's were the ones who were buying groceries.

One Friday at the end of summer in 1939, when Rider was one year old, Grandpa gave in to our pestering and took Jonah, Rider, and me to town for ice cream for the second time in a week.

"Golblast it, this time try to get the ice cream in your mouths instead of on your clothes," he ranted in his oddly companionable fashion as he loaded us into the bed of the truck.

We scrunched down on the pile of old feed sacks, and I held Rider safely between my legs with my arms linked in front of him. When we got to town, we were to wait for Grandpa in the truck while he picked up the mail and then, he said, he would bring us ice cream from Patterson's, the kind that came in small, cardboard tubs with flat wooden spoons.

But when we got to the Municipal Building, a shiny green car sat directly in front, guarded front and back by shiny black cars. Grandpa screeched the truck to a stop.

"Look at that! He's taking over City Hall!" he shouted, and Jonah slid down on the sacks and covered his eyes. The "he" was Pastor Woodie. The green car was his, and the black cars belonged to his deacons, Mr. Arbuthnot and Mr. Scripps.

Grandpa tooted his horn. "Get out here!" he yelled toward the Municipal Building. "Move your dingbusted cars!"

I leaned out of the truck bed, stretching toward Grandpa's open window, hoping to head off a scene. "Patterson will let us park in front of the store if we buy something," I said.

"I don't want to park there!" Grandpa howled. "I want to park where I always park."

The truth is, if the cars had belonged to anyone except Pastor Woodie and the deacons, we already would have been parked in front of Patterson's store. Grandpa had hated the pastor ever since Jonah came to live on the farm, because Woodie said Jonah's birth defects were a punishment from God.

A couple of people came out of Patterson's to stare at us. "What's wrong, Abel?" John Patterson shouted. "What's going on?"

Toot-toot-ta-toot! Grandpa had established a sort of rhythm by then and was not about to abandon his racket. Heads poked out of Julia's Hair Salon and Madame Franchot's Millinery, where the ladies' hats were always on sale. Druid Annie waddled out of the butcher shop, carrying the small package of liver she picked up every day for her cats.

"Abel!" she bawled over the horn and Grandpa's shouts. "Quit that right now."

Grandpa subsided. There were only two people on earth who could get his attention when he was running with a full head of steam. One was Druid Annie and the other was Rider. And Rider, at that moment, was enjoying himself thoroughly.

Druid Annie hoisted her enormous self into the passenger seat of the truck and directed Grandpa across the street. Through the isinglass back window of the truck cab, I saw her whack Grandpa's arm with her rolled-up copy of *Astrological Forecasts for 1939*. "You old sumbitch," she cried. "Why do you aggravate him so much? You want him to bring those women from the county down on you? You know Lara's not up to that kind of trouble."

I didn't know anything about "women from the county,"

but if Druid Annie didn't like them, neither did I. The moment Grandpa parked the truck, Jonah and I piled out of the back and I lifted Rider to the ground.

Jonah beat me to the passenger door and opened it for Druid Annie. "Annie!" he bawled happily. "Whatsa poop?"

"Aw, Abel," Druid Annie yelled at Grandpa, her fat face purple. "Listen to that. That's you talking, not Lara. You got those kids sounding like dirty old men."

"Poop," Rider said obligingly as he smiled at Druid Annie.

"Quit that!" Grandpa yelled at him. "Goldang kids."

We and our language difficulties might have escaped safely inside Patterson's then, if Pastor Woodie had not come out of the Municipal Building and seen our ragged band. "Stop!" he shouted. "You, Abel Chance, stop in your tracks."

"Sneeze and go blind!" Grandpa shouted back and he opened the screen door and swept off his cloth cap. "Inside, ladies." Druid Annie, holding Rider, chugged inside as quickly as her fat little legs would carry her. I followed, colliding with Jonah in the doorway, both of us anxious to avoid Pastor Woodie.

But Woodie followed us, yanking open the screen door and looming in the doorway with the bright noon light behind him, and his silhouette was the dark figure of nightmares. I reached out to touch Rider. Druid Annie looked at me, and I knew that I was not alone with my fears.

"You think driving into town dead drunk and disturbing the peace is setting a Christian example for these children?" Pastor Woodie demanded of my grandfather.

"I'm not drunk," Grandpa said, grinning his awful grin. "Leastways, not yet."

Jonah was making whining noises deep in his throat and plucking a shirt button loose. I took hold of his hand.

"Tell me what you were doing over there at the mayor's office," Grandpa asked Pastor Woodie slyly. "Or maybe you were in Dizzy's office, getting a permit to add on a few rooms to that bordello of yours out in back of the bus station. Is that right, pastor? Expanding your business, are you?"

Millie Little, who'd been buying sliced bread and mayonnaise at the counter, gasped and covered her buck teeth with both hands. But I could see that she was glad Grandpa said what he said.

Druid Annie broke the tension. "Give these kids some of those ice cream cups," she said to John Patterson.

"Let me treat them," Millie offered. "I love that baby, and Rachel helps me with my packages, and Jonah holds the door open for me. Why, I owe them a treat." She was babbling nervously, and Druid Annie and I got right in there and babbled with her.

The pastor left then, and everyone turned a little silly with relief, giggling and hugging. Everyone, that is, but Grandpa and Rider. Grandpa kicked the toe of his boot against a box of early potatoes, his head bent. And Rider looked straight at me, unsmiling. Something caught at my heart, and I longed suddenly and fiercely for my brother's father. If he came to stay with us, Rider would be safe.

But safe from what, I wondered, bewildered by my own

fear. What nameless threat had lingered behind when Pastor Woodie left?

So for the first time in my life I had nightmares, formless tangles of dread and darkness. I came to believe that Rider's father might be an answer to many of our problems. Rider should have a protector. Mama should have a husband. And we could use help at home. I did my best to help Grandpa, and Hank came after school and on weekends, but there was work that never got finished. Some was never even started. We Chances didn't prosper, but barely hung on year after year.

But Mama never mentioned the man. I suppose Grandpa must have asked her, some time or other, who Rider's father was. How she answered him, I could not imagine. She never answered me when I asked, but always told me instead that the situation was "complicated" and "very private."

In September 1939, Mama and I walked the mile to Rider's Dock together each day, she striding briskly toward her job in the dime store at the foot of Front Street near the sound, and I shuffling cheerfully toward school.

One morning a few weeks after Pastor Woodie's disastrous visit, while we were on the edge of town, I glanced over at Mama and said, "Do you ever hear from Rider's father?"

The rhythm of Mama's walk broke, but then she hurried on. "Not very often. Why?"

"Does he know about Rider?" For a moment, while I asked the question, I felt such a surge of hope that the world around me seemed about to burst into an unseasonable spring. Bells and trumpets waited offstage, ready to sound out. He would come, the shining, smiling man, and Rider would be safe.

"No, I didn't tell him," she said.

I slowed my feet. "Don't you think he should know?"

Mama touched her lips with her fingers, as if to keep herself from speaking. "He'd feel so bad because he can't help."

"What do you mean?"

She glanced at me, then looked ahead. "He can't find a steady job, so he moves around with a group of fruit pickers."

I thought this through. "I don't see what that has to do with anything. He could come here and help Grandpa." And marry you, I added silently.

Mama walked faster, and I hurried to catch up. "I'd be afraid to offer him what might seem like charity. Someday things might be different. Hard times can't last forever."

"Well, wouldn't he want his little boy now?" I exclaimed.

"Of course," she said. She blinked rapidly.

"Then write him and tell him about Rider," I said.

"There's nothing he could do about Rider. He'd be so ashamed. He doesn't have any money or a place to live, or even any relatives to help out."

Then I understood and I was appalled. "You mean he doesn't have any place to go back to?" Was that possible? Were there people who really didn't have a home, not any-place at all where they could go if things got bad or they got sick? Or even if they just got lonely and wanted some-one to talk to?

"That's right," Mama said. "He doesn't have anyone."

I could not imagine it. I had not only my family, but

Cousin Samantha and her husband in Eastern Washington, Cousin Barclay in Seattle, and other Chances who wrote long letters to Mama and sent all sorts of homemade gifts at Christmas.

"But he has Rider," I said, desperately. "And you."

"I made a decision," Mama said. "Maybe it was wrong, but it's too late now to change it."

"But — " I began. I could feel my nose turning red, not from the cold but from unshed tears.

"Please don't say any more," Mama said. She cleared her throat. "I'm sorry, Rachel, but you've got to promise me never to talk about this to anyone. It would only stir up trouble, start things that might turn out wrong. We can't know what the future holds for us. Maybe, somehow, Rider and his father will know each other. But this is the wrong time."

We parted without saying goodbye that morning, and I walked so slowly to school that I was late.

When I opened the door to the combined ninth and tenth grade classroom and saw that the kids were saying the Pledge of Allegiance, I waited outside and planned my excuses.

My teacher, Miss Toohey, was new to the small school that year. She was still having difficulty accepting my family circumstances, and sometimes she kept me in at lunchtime to question me about "the baby" and "poor Jonah" and "dear Mr. Chance." That morning she listened sympathetically to my tale of problems at home (which wasn't exactly a lie, since we usually had problems of some kind), but when I took my seat behind Hank Webster, he turned and grinned knowingly at me.

"Turn around," I said, and I jabbed him with my pencil.

His grin was maddening. "I bet you didn't rake out that chicken house last night and Abel made you do it this morning."

"I did it last night," I said.

"Sure you did," he scoffed. "I'll have to do it Saturday, and I've got to fix the leak in the barn roof, too. You're as lazy as Banjo." He turned his back on me.

I opened my mouth, prepared to argue hotly, but Miss Toohey was watching, so I swallowed my protest and slid down in my seat. Across the room, Maysie Clarence, the only other girl in the ninth grade, watched me and curled her lip scornfully.

Maysie allowed Hank to admire her, and he did. She was short-legged and had small, hard-looking breasts — and she always unbuttoned the top buttons of her blouse after she got to school. The five boys in our grade whispered about her and followed her home.

I knew that I, tall and limber, had a soft, more interesting shape, but I hid it under high-necked baggy blouses and sweaters. I bent over my book and hated her. She and her little brother had a father.

Hank, whom Maysie called Henery, had kissed her once. He and I had been mucking out the cow barn on the day he confessed that to me. I swung my shovel at him and he kept his adventures to himself after that. I lay awake that night wondering what it would be like to be kissed by Hank. I wasn't likely to find out. Or to be kissed by anyone else. My prospects in that town were poor.

Even without Rider, the Chance family was barely tolerated in Rider's Dock. With him, we were an open affront to the small town where Pastor Woodie set the rigid standards for family life. The only real friend I had was Gloria Washington, a year older than I, daughter of the piano player Pastor Woodie hated so much, the man who worked in the stockroom at the dime store and played the old piano up front only when a customer wanted to hear the newest sheet music.

But I seldom saw Gloria outside of school after her mother went to the tuberculosis hospital near Seattle. Gloria had three little sisters to care for, in a small, bare house that had no electricity.

"Ten years from now, where do you suppose we'll be?" she asked me dreamily one day while we shared a lunch of cornbread and Mama's good strawberry jam.

"I'll still be on the farm," I said. "I don't ever want to be anywhere else. What about you?"

"I," she said, "will be living in a big house with a nice husband and two children, and I'll have four electric lamps in every room." She laughed and hugged herself. "I'll never have to worry about anything again."

I wished fiercely that day that four lamps in every room could solve the Chance problems.

🦎 Three

Druid Annie and I never talked about it, but I was always certain that she, too, anticipated disaster of some sort that year. I knew the Chances were vulnerable because we were, after all, a family made up of refugees and misfits, well acquainted with untidy predicaments. Annie probably understood how the disaster might come about.

One afternoon in the late, wet spring of 1940, Annie brought an herbal concoction to ease Jonah's latest head cold, and after coaxing a cup of the awful-looking stuff into him, she tucked him in bed and joined Grandpa and me in the kitchen.

"A shot of whiskey does folks more good than that green stuff of yours," Grandpa said as he dumped a generous amount of liquor in his coffee. He was in the mood for an amicable argument.

Druid Annie scowled as she settled herself in the chair opposite him. "I wish you'd quit saying things like that. Leastwise, don't joke about it around town. You know you wouldn't give the children whiskey, and you'd feel better if you gave yourself a little less of it." She screwed the cap on her quart bottle of herbal medicine and put it in her knitting bag.

"Rachel," she said to me then, "pour some hot water into a cup for me and shake the tea ball in it. This weather has settled in my bones."

Grandpa shoved the whiskey toward her. "This will warm you up, old lady."

"I've got enough trouble without that," Druid Annie said.

"God protects drunkards and fools," Grandpa told her.

"I don't see Him protecting you," Druid Annie snapped. "Abel, you'd handle trouble better if you weren't both a drunk and a fool. The rest of the Chances were always satisfied with just being fools."

"What trouble do you mean?" I asked as I put down her tea.

"Never mind Annie," Grandpa interrupted, grinning. "Her folks came from Wales. The Welsh see trouble in every shadow and hear it in the wind. That's because they had legends instead of laws. Americans put our faith in laws instead of old tales about spirits living at the bottom of lakes and fortunetellers in caves. We don't believe in spooks, and the law protects us from the worst of the scoundrels. Yessir." He leveled a sharp look at Annie. "Some of the Chances may be fools, but the rest of us make up for it."

"That's news to those who worry about you," Annie grumbled. "Abel, you've got to be careful . . ."

She broke off because Mama came home then, laughing with pleasure to find Druid Annie there, and no one said another word about the Chance family fools. Mama always fretted and turned pale during conversations about trouble — past, present, or future.

But there was no doubt in my mind that God not only didn't protect my hard-drinking grandfather, He didn't extend much assistance to the rest of the Chances either. I suspected unhappily that maybe we were just too foolish. Like Grandpa, I wasn't a churchgoer, but that didn't mean I didn't do a lot of wondering about things.

We didn't even recognize danger when we saw it. Instead, we viewed with fascinated disgust the arrival of Pastor Woodie's friend, the Reverend Billy Bong, and his campground revival troupe called (for the time being) the Anointed Children of Almighty God.

May brought our first news of their coming. Grandpa, obsessively optimistic in spite of his short temper, decided to take Rider, Jonah, and me to town for ice cream one warm Saturday. The combination of ice cream, a vehicle, and untidy children would have been avoided by anyone else who had Grandpa's regrettable attraction for disaster.

"You, Hank!" he bellowed toward the barn, where Hank was working in the loft. "Get down here and help me keep these kids in line when we get to town. You can ride in front with me."

Hank, fancying himself more man than boy, strutted as he left his work to join us. That left me, jealous and gritting my teeth, to ride in back with Rider and Jonah.

"Don't sing," I growled to Jonah. He had recently been taught "Camptown Races" by Druid Annie. None of the rest of us felt that we owed her gratitude for this because Jonah sang it all day, every day. Even Rider was tired of it.

Grandpa parked in front of the Municipal Building and

limped away without looking back, confident that we would follow him into Patterson's like a line of quail chicks.

Jonah took Rider's hand and started across the street. Hank held out his hand to me, grinning. "Need some help?" he asked.

I was a true Chance woman, not a lady like Mama, and so I socked his arm hard enough to make him wince. "Help Maysie," I said shortly, and I stalked off. I'd never forgotten, or forgiven, what he told me that day in the barn.

He trailed behind me, laughing. He felt superior to me because he was the best student at school. In spite of his family's pressure to find full-time work, he was planning on staying until he graduated. In fact, I'd even heard Grandpa offering Hank the bunk in the barn storeroom if the Websters ever grew too insistent. Grandpa believed in education, even though he'd never gone further than third grade himself. Having Hank living at the farm was not a prospect I could bear to consider, even though I wouldn't have blamed Hank if he'd run away from his jailbird father and the shallow ignoramus who was his mother. If he did run away, however, I wanted it to be in some other direction than ours.

There had been several fly-specked posters in Patterson's dusty window all year long. John habitually forgot to take posters down after the fairs and carnivals they advertised had left town, and the yellowing reminders of our past celebrations stayed in place until the time came when there was no more room for new announcements. John had tidied up since our last visit to town with Grandpa, because now only one poster decorated the window.

"The Devil Is Reaching for You!" the new poster announced in tall black letters with bright red flames licking around them. "Sinners, Run for Your Lives!"

"Aw, Judas Priest," Grandpa said. He had stopped on the porch to stare at the poster, and the rest of us gathered around him. Hank could barely hide his grin. Like Rider, he took unholy delight in Grandpa's harangues. But Jonah and I, for separate reasons, sidled toward the screen door. As simple as he was, Jonah still understood enough to want to get his ice cream and hurry back to the truck, cutting down the chances of attracting attention.

Usually I didn't mind lingering in town, but the poster alarmed me. I was a quick reader, and I had seen what Grandpa had yet to read. Pastor Woodie was assisting in the organized flight from the devil.

Grandpa read aloud, his anger increasing with each word. "'Come to the Rider's Dock campground and hear the Reverend Billy Bong! Throw yourself on the mercy of our Heavenly Father and let the Anointed Children of Almighty God hide you from the Devil beneath their sheltering wings.'" Under the date, in small letters, Pastor Woodie's name appeared as the local sponsor. Grandpa did not read that aloud. Instead, he jerked the screen door open.

John Patterson looked up from the meat slicer, where he was pressing a slab of bacon against the blade. "How are you, Abel?"

"Tell me that I'm imagining things," Grandpa demanded as he stomped across the oiled wood floor. "Tell me that tick-infested Billy Bong isn't coming back to Rider's Dock again."

"He's coming all right." John gathered up thick slices of

27

bacon and dropped them on a piece of paper. "Is this enough for you, Mrs. Jackson?"

Agatha Jackson nodded briskly and opened her black purse. "Afternoon, Abel," she said to Grandpa while she picked through her coin purse. "I just saw Lara at the five-and-dime, and she says your cousin Samantha in Spokane put her father-in-law in the hospital last week. Terrible news."

Grandpa was not about to be distracted with gossip. He nodded brusquely to Mrs. Jackson and leaned over the counter toward John. John was a tall man, but he was still intimidated.

"The last time Billy Bong showed up," Grandpa grumbled, "he had half the dingbusted sheep in this town flopping around on the ground with their eyes rolled back in their heads and the other half over in Pine Valley setting fire to the picture show because *Snow White and the Seven Dwarfs* had a witch in it."

Mrs. Jackson slipped her package into her string bag. "You're working yourself up into apoplexy," she said. "Reverend Billy wasn't to blame for the fire and you know it. And he's not with the same church anymore."

"He's not with any church!" Grandpa kicked the counter for emphasis. "He's not even a genuine goddam reverend. And he changes the name of his traveling loony bin every other month. Just as soon as they get caught picking one pocket, they call themselves something else so that they can get away with picking the other."

John slid the bacon slab back in the small glass case where he kept odds and ends of smoked meats. "Billy's good for business, Abel. Better than the circus. That's so, isn't it, Mrs. Jackson?"

Mrs. Jackson nodded. "Everybody in this end of the county will show up." She rented rooms in her big house, and any form of traveling entertainment, from carnival to tent revival, guaranteed that all her rooms would be taken, as well as every other spare bedroom in town. The people on the north side of Rider's Dock even rented their front yards after the tent sites at the campground filled up. And John Patterson would probably make more money during the revival than he did during the rest of the summer.

Mrs. Jackson left and Grandpa ordered our ice cream, but the subject of Billy Bong and his Anointed Children of Almighty God was not forgotten. While we ate our ice cream in the back of the truck, Grandpa drove around town, up one dusty street and down another, and everywhere we found posters.

Once Hank turned and glanced back at me, a grin twitching the corners of his mouth. I looked away, in time to see a spoonful of ice cream slide off Jonah's wooden spoon and plop on the bed of the truck, between his legs.

"Grab that rag behind you and clean it up," I told Jonah. "I can't help you now. I've got my hands full with Rider." Even while I spoke, I scraped melted ice cream off Rider's chin. My own treat was turning to mush.

Jonah sighed and put his carton of ice cream on his knee and it promptly tipped over. He burst into noisy weeping.

I muttered a few of Grandpa's curses. The truck lurched over a rough place in the road, and through the open window I could hear Grandpa ranting about the infamous Billy

Bong with his long white hair and white suits, and his out-stretched palm.

The revival was a month away. I groaned, thinking about it. Pastor Woodie had left us more or less to ourselves for a while, except for those situations where he and Grandpa came face to face on the street. But I was certain that he hadn't changed his mind about wanting Mama to give Rider up for adoption, and so our temporarily peaceful state would come to an abrupt end if Grandpa erupted over the coming of the Anointed Children.

Why didn't adults learn? Any child worth his weight in gum wrappers could tell you that the best thing to do when you couldn't get along with somebody was stay away from him. As far away as possible. Grandpa and Pastor Woodie seemed as attracted to one another as a magnet and iron filings.

At dinner that night, Grandpa told Mama that Billy Bong was coming.

She was buttering bread for Rider, and she looked up quickly. "Don't aggravate Pastor Woodie over this, Abel," she said. "I'm always hoping he'll forget about us. He hasn't been in the store for weeks, and I'd like to keep it that way."

Hank, who often ate dinner with us when he came to do chores during the week, took a deep swallow of milk and put his glass down with a thump. "Pastor Woodie's got all he can handle right now," he said. He wore a strange, anguished smile. "He's praying over my aunt Betty-Dean these days."

"Aw, blast my eyes!" Grandpa exploded. "Is that no-good Mike Webster knocking her around again?" He slammed the gravy bowl down and gravy slopped over on the tablecloth. Jonah sucked in his breath and Rider stopped chewing.

Hank, staring at his plate, nodded.

I was fascinated. "Your uncle hits your aunt?" I asked. "Does she hit him back?"

"No, of course not," Grandpa interrupted, "and that's why he hits her again. If she'd haul off and knock him over the outhouse once or twice, he'd learn better. Mike Webster was behind the door when the brains were passed out, but he could remember a lump on the skull if you gave him one that was big enough."

Mama was signaling me with her eyebrows, but I ignored her. "Why does your uncle Mike hit his wife?" I asked Hank.

Hank stuffed a large piece of meat in his mouth and chewed. I waited. "Well?" I asked, unable to contain my impatience.

"Rachel," Mama said, warning me, her hands fluttering.

"He hits her because he hits everybody," Hank said finally.

"She ought to hit him back," I said. "Hard."

Mama raised her gaze to the ceiling. "That wouldn't solve anything, Rachel. She'd be as bad as he is, then."

Grandpa and I exchanged a meaningful glance. We weren't passive sufferers like Mama. "If *I* hit him, it would solve things," I said, and Grandpa shouted with laughter.

"That's the Chance in you talking," he said, delighted.

"Anyway," Hank said, "Pastor Woodie's so busy trying

to make Aunt Betty-Dean learn to obey and quit arguing with Uncle Mike that he doesn't have time to worry about Rider right now."

Rider, hearing his name, looked around the table expectantly.

"You're a good boy," Mama said, smiling at him. "Abel," she said to Grandpa, "please don't start up anything. It's not our business if people like those revival meetings."

"They burned down the picture show last time," Grandpa said. "Billy Bong makes everybody crazy."

Mama sighed. "You just keep out of it. They'll only be here one weekend and then everything will be back to normal again. If you don't aggravate Pastor Woodie, that is."

Grandpa grumbled something unintelligible and mopped up gravy from his plate with a bread crust.

From the corner of my eye I saw Hank watching me. The next time we were alone, I was going to ask more questions about his Aunt Betty-Dean. I tried to imagine my own reaction to a husband who beat me and then sent the pastor to lecture me on obedience. Why did she put up with either one of them? There was no understanding adults.

On the day before Billy Bong and the Anointed Children of Almighty God were due, Pastor Woodie personally directed the hanging of large blue banners over the main street in Rider's Dock.

Grandpa drove into town that hot June day to pick up chicken feed, and Hank and I were with him. While Hank loaded sacks on the back of the truck, I watched the long banners hauled into position. "Worship!" proclaimed one.

"Pray!" ordered another. "Repent!" was my favorite, however, because the *p* was backward.

Maysie Clarence minced out of the millinery shop. "Are you going to the revival meeting, Rachel?" she asked when she saw me. She covered her bright-painted mouth with her hand while she giggled. "I won't ask if your mama's going, even though she probably ought to. That's what *my* mama says, anyway"

"I'm too busy," I said innocently. "Hank and I have plans."

We had no plans, of course, nor would we make any, but Maysie's face turned blotchy and that satisfied me.

Riding home, I was squeezed in between Grandpa and Hank on the narrow bench seat in the truck, and they talked the whole time about the price of cracked corn, so I didn't have an opportunity to turn the conversation to the arrival of Billy Bong. I wanted to witness it for myself, but unless this event coincided with Grandpa's trip into town for the mail, there was little chance of it. And even then, he'd have to include Jonah and Rider in the plan, for we couldn't leave the two of them alone and we couldn't always count on Druid Annie being available to babysit them. Her practice of herbal medicine kept her busy.

We were unloading the sacks in front of the shed when I finally got a chance to ask if we could all go to town the next day to see Billy Bong and his white bus arrive. "Rider would love it," I said. Reminding Grandpa of Rider was as good a way of manipulating him as any I'd ever discovered.

"Holy cow," Grandpa complained. "Why do you want to see that hullabaloo?"

Hank's shoulders shook with silent laughter.

"What's so funny?" I demanded.

"You planning on getting religion?" Hank asked as he slung a sack from the truck to the shed.

"I only want to see the parade," I said.

"Well, you'd see Pastor Woodie in his green car and Arbuthnot and Scripps in their black cars, and all of their wives and kids and in-laws and outlaws stuffed inside until the doors won't shut," Grandpa said, "and behind them the mayor and Dizzy Snope with the whole church choir yelling on his flatbed truck. That's not a parade. It's just folks making fools out of themselves."

I ignored him. "And then the big white bus comes?"

"That's the way it was last time," Hank said, "only then Billy Bong called his church the United Heavenly White Brethren."

"What happened to the United Heavenly White *Sistren*?" I asked, smirking. "Or the United Heavenly Colored *Fathren* and *Mothren*?"

"They were all home whipping their Goddam Heavenly *Children*," Grandpa shouted. "You two, get busy. I don't want to hear any more about that goldanged parade."

But from the very way he said it, I knew we were going.

The parade was just as he said it would be, and I was disappointed. The cars drove slowly down the main street, horns honking, and people sauntered out from the stores to watch. Pastor Woodie's congregation threw confetti as the cars went by, which did please Rider.

Three white cars followed, each driven by a sober man in a black suit. In one of them, a flat-faced woman stared hard at Rider, her head turning as she passed. Then the

34

bus came, and the Reverend Billy Bong stood in the open doorway, slowly waving a white hat. He looked the way he had been described to me, tall and heavy, with long white hair. I walked back to the truck, puzzled. This was the man who was supposed to have been such a convincing speaker that men from Rider's Dock had actually burned down a movie theater? I found it hard to believe.

But then, I hadn't yet heard Billy Bong speak.

Altogether, the parade wasn't worth the trip. Ordinarily I would have appreciated any reason to go to town, but I was left uneasy. The feeling had nothing to do with Billy Bong.

When Pastor Woodie passed by, he'd seen the Chance family watching. There was something about the calculating way he'd looked at Rider that raised goose bumps on my arms.

Druid Annie always said that I could "see true," just as she did. She meant that sometimes I knew what was coming. But I pushed down my uneasy feelings instead of dragging them up and sorting them out.

Halfway home, Jonah began singing again, and I sang along with him, my mind on dinner.

❧ Four

Mama was home when we returned to the farm. First we saw the car belonging to Cousin Barclay Chance from Seattle parked in the driveway. That surprised us, for Cousin Barclay visited us only once or twice a year. Next we saw Cousin Barclay himself, red-faced and perspiring, standing on the porch.

"What's going on?" Grandpa demanded.

Cousin Barclay cleared his throat. "Cousin Samantha's father-in-law died. She wants Lara to go to Spokane."

Grandpa pushed by him. "Is she packing? She can make the afternoon train if she hurries."

"We'll catch it in Seattle," Cousin Barclay said, following Grandpa into the kitchen. "I've got to pick up my suitcase."

Jonah, Rider, and I sat down at the table. Hank disappeared the moment he heard that someone had died. His own relatives had short life spans, often dying in colorful and violent ways, and I suspected that he wanted to be clear of the house in case an authority figure of some kind dropped by to ask questions.

Jonah understood that people died, but Rider didn't, so

he looked to me for an explanation of our sudden change in mood.

"Mama has to go on a trip," I said. "She's going bye-bye, but she'll be back soon."

Rider's face puckered. "Pick me up, sis," he wept, raising his arms to me.

I pulled him to my lap. "We'll have ice cream every day," I promised rashly. Rider leaned his head against me and clutched the front of my overalls, his hands looking like small starfish against the faded denim.

Mama carried her suitcase out of the bedroom and stopped when she saw me. "I hate to go, but I trust you to manage," she said, addressing me as the most competent member of the family she was leaving behind. She took Rider, kissed him and put him down, then bent to hug me.

"It'll be for just a few days," she said. "We can't leave the cousins to go through this by themselves. They'll have to leave the farm now and I can't imagine what they'll do. The bank will take the place and throw them off. They'll be out of their minds."

I was appalled at this catastrophe, even though it was not a complete surprise. I knew enough about the extended family's affairs to be aware that the Devereaux farm had been owned by a bank since the year the spring was so wet that the seed rotted in the fields. "They could come here," I said.

Mama put on her summer hat and tucked her fair hair under the brim. "They might." She waited until Grandpa carried her suitcase outside, and then whispered quickly, "Keep him out of trouble if you can. This is a bad time — he hates Billy Bong so much. I don't think I can bear worrying about all of you, too. I'll be back as soon as I can."

She kissed Rider once more. We watched her leave from the porch, and Rider hiccuped softly, his thumb in his mouth.

After the dust settled behind Barclay's car, I put Rider down for his nap on the shady side porch. Hank loped up while I was still sitting on the glider beside Rider, to tell Grandpa that on his way home he'd seen our calf out on the road.

"I caught him and took him back, but that fence has got to be fixed with something better than rope," Hank said.

Grandpa, sipping warmed-over coffee laced with whiskey, grunted. "I hate to turn the cows into the other field. The weather turned so hot that it's dry already, and there's no creek."

Hank shrugged. "What do you want to do?"

Grandpa slammed his cup down on the porch railing and Rider twitched in his sleep. "Put them in the dry field. I'll help. This heat's not good for anything but those crazy blasphemers out at the campground."

As they walked away, I heard Hank ask, "Why is Billy Bong a blasphemer? He talks about God, and Father Gates at the Episcopal church talks about God. What's the difference?"

"Judas Priest!" cried Grandpa. "If you can't tell the difference, stay away from Billy Bong or you'll be rolling around on the ground with the rest of them."

They were still discussing Billy Bong when they disappeared through the trees that ran along the fence separating the yard from the field by the road, where a creek ran all summer. Their voices faded away. Rider slept, his face flushed and damp. A fly buzzed on the wrong side of the screen door, and in the house Jonah sang "Camptown Races" softly as he rocked himself in Mama's chair.

All afternoon Grandpa and Hank drove back and forth between the well and the far field, hauling water in wooden barrels to fill the troughs for our cow and calf, as well as the cows that Millie Little's father boarded with us after his creek went dry each summer.

Then, when the sun was hottest and the sky turned to brass overhead, they drove the truck into town to load up with the material they needed for the overdue fence repairs.

"I hate spending the money," Grandpa complained when they came back with the first load. He rested for a while in the shade on the porch, drinking lemonade, breathing a little too hard. "If it's not one thing, it's six. Your ma's gone and the fence is shot and from the looks of the sky, the whole weekend is going to be hotter than hell."

"I'll help with the fence," I said. "Hank and I can do it."

Grandpa glared at me, his eyes bloodshot. "You keep the boys out of my hair and we'll have it done by Sunday night."

In the distance, I saw the truck parked in the road and Hank dragging posts out of the back. "It's too bad you had to buy those posts," I said.

"I'm too dingdonged old to cut fence posts anymore," Grandpa grumbled. "Listen, we didn't have room for the wire. You go back into town with Hank and get it, and be sure you don't get cheated on the price. But first, stop by Annie's and ask her to come help with the boys. I'm going to dig postholes and I can't watch them."

I was peeling an orange for Rider and I didn't dare look up. "Let Hank dig," I said.

Grandpa didn't answer, but went out to yell for Hank.

Hank and I reached the lumberyard five minutes before it closed. We'd passed the campground on the way there and saw dusty cars parked in crowded rows on all sides of Billy Bong's tent. When we passed it again on the way home, we saw that cars were now parked blocks away, and people streamed along the sidewalks under the drooping branches of old maples.

Hank stopped the truck suddenly. "Let's go have a look."

"Are you crazy?" I exclaimed. "Grandpa will kill us."

"He can't use the wire until we get the posts in and that won't be before tomorrow."

"It's not the wire, it's Billy Bong!" I said. "If Grandpa finds out we went in the tent, he'll have a fit and fall in it."

Hank scratched his elbow thoughtfully. "You didn't see Billy last time he was here, but I did. He's a real hoot."

I considered this. "Do people really roll around on the ground?"

Hank nodded and grinned.

"People we know?"

"Not so many from Rider's Dock," Hank said. "I suppose they wouldn't like it if anybody they knew saw them and talked about it later. But look at all the cars you don't recognize. Strangers from all over the county. They'll really cut loose."

I couldn't resist. Hank parked the truck and we ran back to the campground. We could hear singing from inside the tent and the line outside wasn't as long as it had been when we passed by a few minutes before.

"Do we have to pay to get in?" I whispered.

Hank laughed. "No, but they'll want you to pay to get out."

The tent was as large as a circus tent, filled with folding chairs set in rows. At the side opposite the entrance, Pastor Woodie's choir sang enthusiastically and people fanned themselves with printed programs. A fat lady in a white dress handed each of us a program at the entrance and a scowling man pointed to two seats in a back row. We slipped into our places and slid down, hoping not to be seen. I didn't recognize anyone near us, but a few rows away I saw Agatha Jackson and Hank's Aunt Betty-Dean, who had two black eyes.

Pastor Woodie spoke for a while, a long while, after the choir stopped singing. A few people from out of town yelled "Amen," but nearly everyone else looked bored and impatient. They'd heard everything he had to say a thousand times over. Finally Pastor Woodie introduced the Reverend Billy Bong.

He stepped out from behind a screen that had been set on the stage. The people in the audience stood up and roared. It must have taken two or three minutes for the shouting to stop.

"Beloved sons and daughters," Billy Bong said, "you got here just in the nick of time."

His voice was deep and loving, and he reached toward

us as if he would embrace us. "I'm going to save you from the devil tonight," he crooned, and nearly everyone there shouted, "Amen!"

"Let's go," I whispered. Goose bumps had risen on my arms.

"Wait," Hank said, grinning. "It gets better."

Billy Bong spoke for a long time about the devil and all the interesting things people do when they attract his attention, and then he stepped back and struck a pose, head high, hands clutched together. He was sweating heavily.

"Lord," he cried, "I'm going to tell these children how to escape from the hot, bony hands of Satan, but first, I want them to hear one of your angels sing."

A tall, thin man in a black suit introduced a woman then, Sister Pearl Sweet, the flat-faced woman who'd stared at Rider from one of the cars in the parade.

"She's Billy Bong's sister," Hank whispered. "She's got to be the ugliest woman in the world."

He was right. She was nearly as tall as her brother, but thin as a picket, and her colorless hair was pulled back skin-tight into a knot on the back of her head. She wasn't much of a singer, either. Her voice was remarkable only because it was loud.

While she sang, she watched the two dozen small children sitting on the floor in front of the first row of chairs. They ignored her, but she gave me a chill.

Billy Bong stepped forward again, and he talked and talked until I grew stiff in my chair.

"When do they start rolling around?" I asked Hank.

"Later. After it gets dark outside and just before the guys in the black suits start collecting money."

I stood up. "Let's go. It can't be worth seeing if you have to sit here in this hot smelly tent for another hour."

The people around us glared at us as we made our way to the opening in the tent wall. Two men stood there. "Reverend Bong is still speaking," one said. He blocked the door.

"My sister is going to throw up," Hank said.

The men stepped aside and we ran out into the twilight. A woman stood near the tent, fanning herself, and I recognized her. Pearl Sweet, the singer. She patted her forehead with a handkerchief and I saw her heavy gold wedding ring before she turned away and went back inside the tent.

"What did you think?" Hank asked as we returned to the truck.

"I wish the rolling around had come first, before all the talking," I said.

"But what did you think about what he said?" Hank demanded.

"He sounds like the patent medicine man who came to the farm last spring," I said, "except that he talks about going to hell instead of wasting away with inflammations in your vital organs."

Hank stared at me. "What vital organs?"

"I don't know," I said. "Grandpa threw the salesman out before he told us."

Halfway home I said, "It's going to be dark before we get there and Grandpa will want to know where we were."

"I'll tell him the radiator boiled over on the hill," Hank said readily.

I relaxed. "He'll believe it. The radiator's always boiling over."

The boys were in bed by the time we got home. As predicted, Grandpa was at first furious with us because we were late and then furious with the truck. But he subsided finally and sent Hank home with instructions to return after breakfast the next day.

I found Druid Annie in the kitchen. The remains of her famous boysenberry pie sat on the table.

"I hope Jonah and Rider didn't give you trouble," I told her.

She slid a piece of the pie on a plate and handed it to me. "I kept 'em busy. But your mama's going to scalp me when she gets back." She held up our copy of *Gone With the Wind* and opened it. Several pages were marred with small black handprints.

"What happened?" I asked.

"I took your mama's ink bottle out. I thought I'd write a letter to my sister in Portland while I was here. But I went to check on your grandpa for a minute and when I got back I found Rider had poured the ink out on the floor." She sighed and dropped the book on the table. "The floor cleaned up real nice, but I don't think there's much I can do about the book."

"At least Jonah didn't join in."

"Oh, he did. But he put all his handprints on the table and the ink came right off that oilcloth."

"Maybe I'll cut out one of those handprints and put it in a frame. Mama might like that."

"You're a good daughter, Rachel," Druid Annie said. "But not too good. I heard you telling Abel that the radiator boiled over and that's what took you so long. Now tell me the real story."

I looked up, straight into her bright eyes. "Hank and I went to hear Billy Bong."

"Oh, my word. Why'd you do something like that?"

I shrugged. "I don't know. We didn't stay for the rolling around part, though. Why does everybody get so excited over him?"

"When people get bored, they look for something to do. They aren't always too particular about what it is."

"If that's all it is, why does Grandpa get so mad?"

"He's lived long enough to see how far things can go. You've heard Abel tell about the time some of the men got so excited that they went into Pine Valley in the middle of the night and burned down the picture show. They were sure the devil was responsible for the movies."

"Well, I bet they felt like idiots the next day," I said.

"Maybe a few did. But most didn't. Some people are happiest when they're following a leader who does a lot of punishing. That makes them feel justified in their own meanness."

I scraped the last of the pie off my plate. "Did you ever see Billy Bong?"

She glanced toward the door. "Once." She grinned. "I thought he was just plain silly. And that sister of his has a voice that ought to be used for calling home the cows."

I nodded. "I saw her tonight, too. Pearl Sweet."

"Well, pity her. Her husband's the treasurer for Billy Bong, no matter what he calls his organization, and I've heard that he's a cold man. And she's barren, poor thing. Maybe if she had a child she'd learn to sing a little sweeter."

Grandpa came in then and gave Druid Annie a ride home. While he was gone, I thought about Billy Bong and his mournful sister. Druid Annie was kinder than I, I concluded, because I was certain that not even the presence of a child could improve that voice.

I cut out one of Rider's handprints to frame for Mama and another for me, just to keep. When I was done, I tiptoed around the house tidying up the way Mama always did before she went to bed. I'd done that when she was in Spokane the last time.

Maybe, I thought, smiling as I went up to my room, she'll see Rider's father there this time, too. And bring him home with her.

That happy thought accompanied me into my dreams that night. It was the last peaceful sleep I'd have for a long time.

✿ Five

By five-thirty on Saturday morning, Grandpa and Hank were working on the fence. I heard their voices distantly through my open bedroom window while I lay dozing until Rider woke.

By early afternoon they'd finished digging the new postholes and they came up to the house for a late lunch. Pastor Woodie arrived while we were still sitting at the picnic table in the cool green shade under the big maple.

Banjo, who couldn't remember from one day to the next that he wasn't allowed to sleep on the sofa, remembered Pastor Woodie and crawled under the porch, where he lay barking in the dark. Jonah, humming nervously, lifted Rider to his lap. Grandpa ignored both Pastor Woodie's car and Pastor Woodie. Instead, he helped himself to the last of the watermelon.

Pastor Woodie glared at Hank. "I've got private business with the Chance family," he said.

Hank rested his elbows on the table, making himself comfortable. He smiled unhelpfully at Pastor Woodie.

"Have another glass of lemonade," Grandpa said to Hank.

"Go home," Pastor Woodie told Hank.

Hank looked to Grandpa for instructions. "Stay," Grandpa said. Hank poured himself another glass of lemonade.

Pastor Woodie adjusted his hat. "All right, Abel. Have it your own way. I guess it won't matter if Henry hears what I've got to say to you. The Webster family and the Chance family have got at least one thing in common. You don't care if you make public spectacles of yourselves."

Hank's face turned hard as stone, but Grandpa sucked in his breath and scowled. "Get yourself out of here before I take a shovel handle to you."

Pastor Woodie advanced on us instead. "I hear Lara's gone to Spokane again."

Grandpa nodded shortly.

"We'll pray that she doesn't bring down any more disgrace on you," Pastor Woodie said, with a significant look at Rider.

Grandpa rose. "Lara never brought disgrace on me," he said quietly. I was too scared to breathe, and Jonah hugged Rider until he squeaked. "If you say anything like that to me again, Woodie," Grandpa went on, "I'll make you wish you'd never been born."

Pastor Woodie swallowed hard, but he was determined to have his say and so he scowled and stuck out his chest. "I've told you before that there are people in town who don't think this is a proper place for children. The good ladies from the county welfare office said if there were any more complaints, they might have to put the baby and that girl there into the orphanage in Seattle. And, of course, everybody knows your dummy ought to be sent to an institution."

"Liar," Grandpa said, but I couldn't tell if he meant it.

I, whom Woodie was calling "that girl there," could keep silent no longer. "We aren't orphans!" I shouted. "We've got a home!"

Pastor Woodie pretended that I hadn't spoken. "It's the baby we worry most about, Abel. If Lara would take my advice — "

"She's not giving him away," Grandpa said. "Now turn around and get out of here. Get off my land and don't ever come back. If you do, as God is my witness, I'll shoot you as a trespasser."

"I'm giving you your last chance, Abel," Pastor Woodie said. "There are wonderful people in town for the revival. Some of them could take that baby and give him a proper Christian home. Get Lara back here before it's too late and — "

"You want her to give Rider away like a puppy?" Grandpa asked scornfully. "I doubt that that's what the county busybodies have in mind. Hank, get my shotgun down off the wall in my bedroom and bring it here to me."

Hank got up and sprinted toward the house. His grin was searing and joyful.

Pastor Woodie backed toward his car. "Think about it, Abel."

"I'm thinking that I'm going to shoot you," Grandpa said.

Pastor Woodie opened his car door. "You're making serious trouble for yourself."

Hank leaped off the porch, shotgun in hand. Jonah moaned softly and rocked Rider to and fro.

Pastor Woodie started his car just as Hank handed the shotgun to Grandpa.

"Grandpa, don't," I said. My mouth was dry.

Grandpa raised the shotgun and Pastor Woodie stepped on the gas. Gravel flew from under his tires and spattered on the lawn.

"Doodah, doodah," sang Jonah, his voice trembling.

Hank laughed. "You showed him, Abel. He won't be back."

Grandpa lowered the gun. "Yes, he will," he said. "We're unfinished business for him. Rachel, take Rider to Annie's and use her phone. Ring up Cousin Barclay's house and see if his wife stayed behind when he and Lara left. You and Rider can stay with her until your mama gets back. Then we'll see what we do next."

Hank drove us. The walk was too far on a hot day. We didn't say much, and even Rider seemed apprehensive, even though he couldn't have known what was wrong.

Druid Annie made the call for us. I wasn't very experienced using a telephone, and the operator's pert "Number please?" always caused me to stutter. Cousin Barclay's wife answered the phone after what seemed an eternity. Druid Annie explained the situation.

Hank and I listened to her say, "That's awful!" and "You've got your hands full," and "Well, you're right about that."

What else can go wrong? I thought, despairing.

Druid Annie hung up the phone. "You can't go there," she said flatly. "All three of Barclay's boys got the mumps."

"I've already had mumps," I said. And then I remembered. "But Rider hasn't."

"You can't stay with me," she said. "Agatha Jackson's sister is my neighbor and she snoops and tattles about everything. If you stay here, Pastor Woodie'll hear about it before the day is over." She took Rider and cuddled him to her shoulder. "Let me think. There has to be a safe place for you until Lara comes home."

"I'll stay at the house with them," Hank said suddenly.

"Well, boy, what good do you think that's going to do?" Druid Annie exclaimed. "Your temper is almost as bad as Abel's. What we need now are cool heads and good plans. Once Lara's back, things will look better. And if a businessman like Cousin Barclay speaks up for her, that might quiet those county snoopers."

"Then let's tell her to come back," I said. "There's no phone at Cousin Samantha's, but we could write a letter. Maybe we can't make the post today but it'll be picked up Monday morning. Mama could be on the train by Wednesday."

"But that's four days away," Hank said.

Annie bit her lip while she thought. "Those county women probably don't work on weekends, so Pastor Woodie won't have anybody to tell his lies to until Monday. By then I can find a place for you. Maybe my niece in Seattle can take you in for a while. I'll take the bus in tomorrow morning and talk to her."

"Meanwhile, we'll go back home," I said decisively. I felt better already. "I'll get our clothes ready."

"Abel can drive you in tomorrow night," Druid Annie said. "If it all works out, that is. And I'm sure it will."

Hank drove us back to the farm then, and we explained about Barclay's sons and Druid Annie's plan for Rider and me.

Grandpa considered the news. "That'll have to do, I guess," he said finally. But I saw that he was worried.

He and Hank went back to work on the fence, and the boys and I sat on the cool porch with Banjo. Jonah and Rider slept after a while, and I wanted to, but my clattering thoughts wouldn't let me.

I gathered up all of Rider's clothes and enough of my own to last several days, and packed them in the wicker trunk we used to store our winter blankets. Druid Annie's niece was a stranger to us, but if she'd take us in for a while, I wanted to be as prepared as I possibly could be. I packed two of my favorite books and some of Rider's toys, too.

Hank went home after dark and Grandpa came in, exhausted.

"We should have the fence finished by noon tomorrow," he said after he'd poured himself a generous drink. "Annie will be back by then. If it's all right for you to stay in Seattle, I'll take you there myself. It would be a long bus ride for a little feller like Rider."

I nodded. "Druid Annie says that Cousin Barclay should be able to help with the county people. If there's really any trouble, I mean."

Grandpa didn't respond. He folded both his hands around his glass and stared at the wall. After a long time, he said, "I never could figure out why some people can't leave other people alone. I've even wondered if maybe they've got ticks or tapeworms, something like that. Ticks and tapeworms can turn a dog mean."

He gulped his whiskey and wiped his mouth on the back of his hand. "Then again, most men aren't worth as much as good dogs. Could be some are just born with rotten hearts, like saplings growing too close to a bog. We've got to be thankful this isn't Nazi Germany and we've got laws to protect us."

"Sure," I said.

"But," Grandpa said, "until we need the laws, we'll take care of ourselves."

I didn't sleep well that night, and my dreams were filled with shadows and distant voices calling out garbled warnings. And rotting, spindly trees that toppled toward me.

Druid Annie didn't return until midafternoon on Sunday, and her news was bad. Her niece was leaving on Monday for Chicago, to visit her husband's family. Annie had missed the first bus back to Rider's Dock and had spent her hours at the bus station calling boarding houses she'd found listed in the Seattle papers.

"There's one that didn't sound too bad, Abel," she said. She pulled a scrap of paper from her purse and read from it. "This woman says she can take two children for a few days, especially since Rachel's nearly fifteen."

She folded up the paper and put it back in her purse. "The other places sounded so risky."

Grandpa slammed his glass down on the table. "By God, I'm not going to let these children be driven out of their own home by that pack of meddling troublemakers. I've changed my mind. The kids stay here, and be damned to anybody who tries to take them away!"

Druid Annie patted her forehead with a handkerchief. "Abel, I'm sorry I couldn't be of more help. I stopped by and told Millie Little what was going on. She says if there's anything she can do, just call on her. She's going to talk to Father Gates at the Episcopal church."

"Woman, is there anybody in town you didn't tell?" Grandpa shouted.

"I told the people who'll help you if they can!" Annie shouted back. "You don't have many friends, Abel Chance, and you should be grateful that anyone cares what happens to your family."

Grandpa gulped down the last of the whiskey in his glass. "You did fine, old lady. Judas Priest, it's hot in this room. Rachel! Do we have to have all the windows shut?"

The windows were open, but I got up from the table and shoved them up as high as they'd go. Outside on the porch, Jonah was singing "Camptown Races" and Rider was sharing an oatmeal cookie with Banjo. In the distance, heat shimmered over the road that led to Rider's Dock and beyond to the campground revival.

Reverend Billy Bong and the Anointed Children of Almighty God would be leaving Rider's Dock soon. The immediate threat to Rider would go with them when those "wonderful people" who wanted to give him a home packed up their belongings and followed Billy Bong out of town.

Then all we'd have to contend with would be Pastor Woodie and the women from the county.

That night Jonah wouldn't sleep alone in his own bed, but wept until Grandpa let him carry his pillow and blanket to the living room, where he made a bed for himself on the couch. Rider whimpered for half an hour before he finally dropped off, and I lay awake most of the night, listening. I don't know what I expected to hear. Before dawn I slept hard, and I didn't wake until late. And then it was to Grandpa's shouting.

"Fire!" he yelled from the porch. "Rachel, the field's burning!"

I leaped from bed and yanked up my shade. Smoke boiled over the trees, and I could hear the cows bellowing. Grandpa always herded them from the barn to the field after the early milking, and now they were trapped inside the fences.

I ran downstairs and grabbed Rider out of his crib in Mama's bedroom. Jonah was sitting up on the couch, trembling, clutching his blanket to his chest. I thrust Rider at him.

"Watch him," I said. "I'll help Grandpa get the cows out of the field."

Jonah wailed in terror, but I didn't have time to reassure him. I ran out after Grandpa, wearing nothing but my short summer nightgown and my old leather slippers. Ahead of me, Grandpa stumbled over the dry ground. The cows bellowed urgently. My eyes already stung from the smoke.

There's nothing that scares a farmer more than a fire in a dry field where stock are pastured. Unless it's a fire in a barn.

The smoke was blowing toward us, and the cows lumbered ahead of it and the flames that rolled lazily at their heels. I reached the gate before Grandpa, slipped up the wire loop that held it shut, and ran toward Lizabet, our Jersey, who led the others. She lumbered faster when she saw me, and her calf trotted nervously at her side.

"Come, Lizabet," I said, trying to sound calm, even though the smoke was choking me. "It's all right. I'm here now."

She saw the open gate and Grandpa, running toward it on the other side. I slapped her flank as she passed me. The other cows followed, rolling their eyes at me. They didn't know me very well and they probably regarded me as one more threat.

Grandpa turned Lizabet down the length of the newly fenced field toward the far gate, the one that led to the barnyard. The cows passed him, trotting.

"Rachel!" Grandpa shouted. "Drive them into the garden."

They'd eat everything, but what did it matter? They'd be safe. The garden was fenced and it was on the other side of the house from the fire. Surely it wouldn't burn that far, I told myself. There was all the bare ground between the barn and the house to act as a firebreak.

I chased after the cows, shouting, and when I looked back, I saw Grandpa stumping for the chicken house. The chickens would be safe enough out in the yard, but it was possible that some might have been inside in the laying boxes.

Lizabet slowed to a walk and let me shove her toward the garden gate. Once she saw where she was going, she hurried again, and the other cows followed agreeably enough. I pushed the gate closed behind them and tried not to think of the lettuce and early peas we wouldn't be seeing on our table.

I turned back toward the house. The smoke from the field didn't seem any worse than before, and the weak wind had died down. I couldn't see flames from where I was, so the fire was going out. We might escape without too much harm.

I opened the back door, calling out, "Jonah? Everything's all right now."

He didn't answer me. I stopped at the sink and splashed cold water over my face and hair. My eyes still stung from the smoke.

"Jonah, you don't need to be scared," I called out to him. "The fire's going out and Grandpa will be here in a minute."

No answer.

Curious, I hurried toward the door that led to the living room, wiping water from my eyes as I went. "Jonah?"

He wasn't there.

"Jonah!" I shouted, alarmed now, starting for the stairs. "Jonah, answer me. You're scaring me."

I ran up the stairs and looked in his room, then mine. Not there. I rushed back down to Mama's room, then Grandpa's.

"Rider? Jonah? Don't hide from me now. It's not funny!"

I ran through the kitchen to the living room. I had a stitch in my side and my chest hurt. "Jonah! Rider! Don't tease me."

The house was empty. I ran out the front door, and the screen door hit the siding with a crack like a shot. Where was the dog?

"Banjo!" I screamed.

Grandpa was running from the chicken coop. "What's wrong? Where are the boys?"

I heard Banjo whining under the porch. I dropped to my knees and looked. There, in the dark, Banjo and Jonah huddled together.

I swallowed. "Where's Rider?" I asked, my voice shaking.

Jonah shook his misshapen head. His eyes were swollen from crying and his nose ran.

I reached out to him. "It's okay. Whatever happened, we'll fix it. You come out to Rachel now and tell me where Rider is."

But Jonah drew back from me.

I reached farther under the porch and grabbed his arm. "Jonah! What's happened to Rider! Where is he?"

"Oh, sweet Jesus," Grandpa said. He knelt down beside me awkwardly. "Jonah, where's Rider? You got to tell us now."

"Gone," Jonah wept. He hid his face. "Gone."

❧ Six

I had never deluded myself by thinking that the Chance family was widely respected in Rider's Dock, but until my brother was stolen I never knew how few people were willing to stand with us.

No, that's unjust. I suppose most people were shocked and upset. But the truth was that Mama's fatherless child was the town's favorite scandal. Rider's disappearance was exactly the sort of thing they felt the Chances deserved. And, of course, they were very glad that one of their own hadn't attracted the attention of strangers.

But there were some who cared. As soon as Grandpa untangled Jonah's confused and halting story, he ran for the truck, his destination Annie's house and her telephone.

"Those men can't have gone very far," he shouted at me as he climbed into the truck. "The police will catch them before they get out of town."

I watched him drive away, and I kept nodding my head long after he was out of sight. Of course, he was right. The men Jonah described as strangers, the men he said wore black coats, who had slapped him until he let go of

Rider — oh, they'd be caught and punished and frightened and hurt. Yes, hurt! I clenched my fists and remembered with pleasure the movies I'd seen where the police drew guns from holsters and shot evil men.

While I waited for news, I dressed and fixed breakfast for Jonah, but he wouldn't eat. He rocked in Mama's chair and moaned.

I fed the chickens and watched the road. No one came. Restless, I wandered to the garden fence and saw that Lizabet and her friends had already eaten the peas and were happily feasting on green tomatoes. The summer morning smelled of smoke.

Still Grandpa did not return. I fed Banjo and swept the kitchen.

Hank hurried in, letting the screen door bang behind him. "The dry field's burned and half of the good one's ruined," he said. "What happened?"

"My brother is gone," I told him. "While Grandpa and I were driving the cows away from the fire, some men came and took Rider."

Hank stared at me. "That's crazy. Who'd steal the kid?"

Jonah moaned and rocked faster.

I told the story, for if I'd left it to Jonah, the telling would have taken as long as it did the first time. "Jonah heard a car in the driveway and saw some men in it. Two of them came to the door. They looked scary to Jonah, so he took Rider out the back door and was going to find us, but they heard him and stopped him. They hit him until he let go of Rider. They put Rider in the car and drove away with him."

"Who were they?" Hank asked. "Did they start the fire?"

"Jonah didn't know them. Men in black suits, he said. I suppose they started the fire to get us out of the way."

Jonah rocked faster. "*He* was in the car," he said, weeping.

I bent to hug him, and he clamped his arms around my waist. "We'll get him back," I said, thinking he meant Rider. "We'll take him back out of that old car, you just wait."

"No, no," Jonah bawled. "*He* was in the car. *He* was."

"Yes, but we'll get him back." I asked Hank to bring me a glass of water for Jonah.

"No, *he* was in the car. Woodie, Woodie, Woodie!"

Hank and I stared at each other.

"What's he talking about?" Hank asked hoarsely.

I knelt beside the chair. "Do you mean that Pastor Woodie was in the car with the men who took Rider?" I asked Jonah.

"Rider cried!" Jonah shouted, and he began weeping hysterically then. We knew we wouldn't get anything else out of him until he quieted down.

"He doesn't know what he's talking about," Hank said. "Pastor Woodie couldn't be that stupid. Abel would kill him for sure."

"Stay here and watch Jonah," I said. "I'm going to run to Druid Annie's and tell Grandpa."

I was halfway out the door when I saw that Druid Annie was coming across our yard, trotting as fast as she could. She saw me and waved.

"What's wrong?" I cried.

Druid Annie climbed the porch steps, wheezing faintly. "This is terrible, terrible! Abel drove to town to see Pete

Carmichael. Pete doesn't believe what Jonah saw, and he said on the telephone that Rider's probably hiding somewhere or maybe lost and Jonah's lying to save his skin."

Pete Carmichael was the police chief in Rider's Dock and a member of Pastor Woodie's church. I didn't admire the chief any more than Grandpa did, but I couldn't imagine him not caring about a missing child. But probably he did believe that Jonah was somehow responsible. It was easy to blame someone like Jonah for anything that happened.

I told Druid Annie what Jonah had said about Pastor Woodie

She'd eased herself down into a chair and was mopping her forehead with her handkerchief. "Aw, Jonah must be mistaken. Pastor Woodie is a meddling troublemaker, but I can't believe that he'd take Rider. What would he do with him? Everybody in town knows Rider by sight, so the Woodies couldn't keep him."

"Pastor Woodie threatened to ask the county to put Rider and Rachel in the orphanage in Seattle," Hank said. "Maybe he took Rider there."

"But not like this!" Annie protested.

"Grandpa never would have let him do that," I said. "Woodie knew he'd have to steal Rider if he wanted to put him in that orphanage!"

"But he can't get away with it," Annie said firmly. "There are laws! All kinds of 'em. Nobody can just walk in and take a little boy."

"The women from the county walked in and took my aunt Betty-Dean's two boys," Hank said dismally.

"That was for good reason," Annie said. "And they didn't go to the orphanage. They went to a foster home.

You know your uncle had been abusing those boys. The county did right, except that it broke Betty-Dean's heart. But this is different. Rider has a loving family and a good home." She wiped tears from her eyes. "There are laws to prevent people from taking children."

"Well, I guess the laws don't work then!" I cried furiously. "Because somebody came here this morning and hit Jonah and stole Rider. And they weren't women. They were men in black suits . . ."

I looked at Hank and found him looking at me. Neither of us blinked. "Billy Bong's men," Hank said, and his voice cracked.

"Pastor Woodie said that there were people who'd come to town with Billy Bong who would give Rider a home," I babbled to Annie. "They took Rider. They must have."

"Abel's got to hear this," Annie said. She would have trotted back home to her phone then, but Grandpa drove up, followed by Pete Carmichael in his police car.

We told them. Grandpa believed us and howled like a madman, but Pete Carmichael rolled his eyes and sighed.

"That's just plain stupid," he told Hank and me. "You can't go around starting rumors like that! We got to get sense out of Jonah and find out what really happened."

He strutted toward the cowering Jonah, one hand resting on his holstered gun. "You quit lying now, boy, and tell us what happened. Don't go blaming anybody else. You weren't watching Rider and he wandered off, didn't he?"

Jonah clapped one hand over his eyes and the other over his mouth. Nothing Chief Carmichael said could persuade him to answer, and after a while the man left in disgust.

He returned an hour later with a dozen men from town

who searched the farm from the cellar in the house to the loft in the barn and backward and forward across the fields. Rider wasn't there. And they lost the precious time that could have been spent pursuing Reverend Billy Bong and his Anointed Children of Almighty God. By then, I was absolutely convinced that Rider was with them.

While Chief Carmichael was in town raising the search party, another proven friend arrived. Millie Little heard about Rider's disappearance from Agatha Jackson, and she drove up in her father's ancient roadster.

"Does Lara know yet?" she asked quickly.

"We have to find Rider first!" I cried. "We can't tell Mama that he's not back yet."

"Millie, there's no telephone at the Devereaux farm," Annie said, ignoring me. "We could send a telegram, though."

"Oh, that's going to take hours, and we can't let her come back alone on that long train trip," Millie cried. "I'll drive to Spokane and get her. Papa and I have been back and forth a hundred times to see his sister, and I know the way by heart. I won't stop for anything but gas."

"I'll get her!" Grandpa shouted. "No woman's going to drive over the pass alone if I have anything to say about it!"

"Well, you don't have anything to say about it!" Millie yelled, surprising us all. "Papa said I could and I will."

And she did. Late the next night she brought Mama home to devastating disappointment. We'd all been certain that one way or another we'd have Rider back by then. But nothing happened, and our frenzied appeals to the police for news resulted only in glib assurances that "everything was being done."

Mama ran in the house, her face white and her hair disheveled. "Where is he? Is he back yet? Where's my baby?"

I will never forget the look on her face when we told her that we still didn't know.

As the days passed, other good and kind people came, people who believed Jonah. Gloria Washington and Sam, her father, brought fresh baked bread and a bowl of chocolate pudding. They begged us to tell them how they could help and wept over silent, suffering Mama, who stood at the window watching, watching.

Millie Little's father ploughed the burned field and reseeded it, working quickly, without speaking to anyone except Hank, who helped him.

Old Melvin Morris, the pharmacist whose foolish wife, Connie, had given Billy Bong their life savings a few years before, persuaded Chief Carmichael that he would be wise to at least investigate our claim that Rider had been stolen by the Anointed Children of Almighty God. Melvin hated Billy Bong as much as Grandpa did, and he'd spent years trying to get back the money his wife had given to Billy Bong when he was calling his people the United Heavenly White Brethren.

"Did Pete believe you?" Grandpa asked Melvin.

Melvin shrugged. "He wasn't really convinced, but he has to pursue it. I warned him how bad he'd look if he didn't even try. Pastor Woodie's been filling his head with rubbish about how Billy Bong could sue Rider's Dock for slander, but I'm sure he's going to follow through." He clapped Grandpa on the shoulder. "You'll get your grandson back."

"The way you got your money back?" Grandpa asked sadly.

Melvin went away with tears in his eyes.

One sultry afternoon Chief Carmichael came to tell us that the Anointed Children of Almighty God had moved down the coast to California. Billy Bong and his trusted assistants had all been contacted, however, and they insisted that there was no one associated with them who would take a child, even an illegitimate child living in an unfit home.

"They said," Chief Carmichael went on doggedly, exasperated with our protests, "that if they'd wanted the child, they would have waited until the boy had been taken away by the county and then they would have applied for adoption at the orphanage. And they want you to understand that they can't be responsible for anything that was done by the people who came to the revival."

"Like they weren't responsible for burning down the picture show," Grandpa shouted. "Didn't anybody go to wherever they're staying and search? Did you just take their word for it?"

"Abel, I got in touch with police everywhere between Rider's Dock and Bakersfield where the Anointed Children stopped. Rider's not with them. You have to face up to it."

"What about Woodie?" Grandpa shouted. "Do you believe his story that he was nowhere near here that morning? Jonah saw him!"

66

Chief Carmichael's gaze slid past us. "You know Jonah's not even as smart as that dog over there. Who knows what he saw? Or what he did."

Grandpa clenched his fists. "If I ever hear you say anything like that again, I'll crack your skull!"

Chief Carmichael hooked his thumbs in his belt. "Calm down. I suppose it's possible that Jonah didn't have anything to do with Rider disappearing. But you got to look at this thing sensibly, Abel. There's nothing more I can do that I haven't already done. We sent out the boy's description from here to Los Angeles and back East, too. Now you got to face up to facts. Maybe you won't see Rider again. If he's been stolen — if! — then we'll all hope and pray that he's with nice folks who can give him a good life."

"A crime's been committed here, Pete," Grandpa said harshly. "If you won't do your duty, I'll find somebody who'll do it for you. Now get off my porch before I knock you off it."

Chief Carmichael left, and I saw the expression of relief on his face. If he'd dared, he would have dusted his hands together and told us that sometimes things happen for the best.

At that time he had what probably seemed to him to be a bigger problem. Hank's uncle, Mike Webster, was taken to jail the same week Rider was stolen. He had not only beaten his wife again, he'd put her in the hospital for several days, too. The troubles of the Webster family were about to eclipse ours.

Early in the evening after Chief Carmichael's last visit to us, Betty-Dean Webster killed her husband with a shotgun, and the disappearance of a small, illegitimate boy no longer interested anyone except our friends. The rest of the town went wild.

Everyone acknowledged, of course, that Mike Webster had been the meanest man in the county. But a man's wife had no right to kill him. It set a bad example, other men said, and crowds gathered outside the jail in the basement of the Municipal Building to stare in silence at the barred window of Betty-Dean's cell.

On the following Sunday, Mama got up early. "God is punishing me," she said when I came into the kitchen to see what was wrong.

She was already dressed, wearing her very best skirt and a soft white blouse. I saw for the first time that there were strands of gray hair mixed in with her curls.

"Where are you going?" I asked as she pulled on the jacket that matched her skirt.

"To church," she said. She hadn't been to any church since Pastor Woodie fired her.

"Not to Pastor Woodie's church!" I begged. "Don't go back there."

Mama's mouth trembled. "I'm going to the Episcopal church. Father Gates told me that they're having special prayers for Rider today. I'm going to pray with them."

She left, and I went to Druid Annie's. I needed to talk to someone besides Grandpa.

"Why does Mama think that God is punishing her?" I asked as Annie fixed us a pot of strong tea.

"Your mama's looking for a reason for losing Rider," Annie told me. She wept, and her tears dropped, hissing, on the stove. "Don't fuss at her. She's blaming herself because

68

she believes that things could have been different, that maybe she could have prevented what happened."

"I don't know what she could have done," I said. I took cups down from the cupboard and put them on the table, then sat down.

Annie poured the tea. "If she faces up to the truth that she couldn't have stopped what happened, she'll feel so helpless that she'll go crazy. Lara isn't strong."

We sipped our scalding tea in silence for a moment.

"When trouble comes," Annie said, "we're going to be alone in the dark with it until it lets go of us. *If* it lets go of us. But we're afraid of knowing that we can't control everything, so we invented guilt and a god who does favors in exchange for terrible sacrifices."

"Then what are we supposed to do?" I asked.

Annie looked at me over the edge of her cup. "We, the strong ones, go to war with the pain. And take our chances."

When we finished our tea, Annie read my fortune in the wet leaves that clung to the bottom of my cup.

"You're going to have a life of adventure," she said solemnly.

"Do the tea leaves say that we'll get Rider back?" I asked.

"Rachel, don't ask me something like that," she cried. "You know my fortunetelling's half fake."

"But you see true most of the time!" I argued.

"And so do you, my girl. *Will* you get Rider back?"

My eyes filled with tears. "I don't know," I whispered. "I'm afraid to know."

We hugged each other, and I dragged home. The scent of fear was sharp in the air. Peace had departed with Rider.

✿ Seven

Druid Annie and Millie Little came to see us one afternoon after a strange series of violent wind- and rainstorms had howled through town. They left their umbrellas on the porch and apologized for their wet shoes.

"This is the worst July I can remember," Millie said as I closed the door behind them. "I suppose we'll have a heat wave next."

Annie hung their coats on the pegs in the kitchen, then came back and sat across from Grandpa. "Lara's working at the dime store again today?"

"She says she feels better if she has something to do," I said. "But she's not waiting on customers much. Mostly she works in the back office. They put her there because she starts crying and it's bad for business."

"Some places would just have fired her," Millie said. She exchanged a glance with Druid Annie.

"How's your leg, Abel?" Annie asked abruptly, as if to change the subject.

"I'm thinking I might cut it off and grow a new one," he said. "It'll keep hurting until this weather breaks."

"I could fix you a poultice to draw the pain," Annie said.

"Be damned to your poultices and nostrums and all the rest of your witch's brews." He fixed his glare, then, at Millie. "Sit down. You make me nervous standing around on one leg like a chicken on a cold morning."

Millie sat hastily.

"Now," Grandpa said. "What's the poop, ladies? You didn't come here to ask about my leg."

"It's Lara," Annie said. She and Millie exchanged another quick, significant look. "This is hard to say, Abel. Millie and I went to town for our groceries this morning, and Chief Carmichael stopped us outside the store and told us that something has to be done about her."

They didn't notice me standing there, listening, folding the dish towel into smaller and smaller squares. What had Mama done? She'd been so silent, so withdrawn, that a sort of tension had built up in me and nothing would have surprised me.

"She's been going to the chief's office every day to ask about Rider," Millie said.

"Pete says that she's driving them wild," Annie went on. "She always says the same thing. 'Did you find my boy yet?' And when they tell her there's no news, she cries. She doesn't say a word, just looks at them with tears running down her face. Sometimes they call over to the dime store and get Sam Washington to fetch her."

I could see that Grandpa was listening carefully, but his face was expressionless. Finally, he said, "She's got a right to ask the police questions ten times a day if she wants to. That's what they're there for."

Annie leaned forward. "Abel, they think she's going

crazy. Pete said if you don't keep her away from there, he'll have to do something drastic."

Grandpa slammed his fist on the table so hard that Jonah, upstairs in his room, began wailing. "He's going to *do something*? Why in hell doesn't he *do something* to find Rider, then? Woodie knows where he is! Billy Bong knows! I say let Pete Carmichael do his duty and make those men tell us where that baby is!"

They couldn't dispute that. But the problem of Mama's visits to the police remained. No one knew how to tell her to stop.

Grandpa, champion of the idea of law and order, decided after that to approach the problem from a new way. "I'm going to force Pete to do his job," he said, and if Pete Carmichael had seen the look in Grandpa's eyes, he wouldn't have slept well.

Grandpa began his letter writing campaign then. He wrote first to the county council, complaining that no one looked for Rider any longer, that the police cared more about the death of a sadistic drunk than they did about the plight of a stolen child.

The county forwarded his letter to Chief Carmichael, who promptly confronted Grandpa with what he called "treachery."

Undaunted, Grandpa wrote to the governor of the state. He received in return the governor's sorrowful assurance that he would personally encourage a thorough investigation of Rider's disappearance. Grandpa's letter was forwarded to Chief Carmichael.

"Abel," the chief shouted, "if you don't quit this letter writing, I'm going to have to take serious steps."

"Off the end of the old dock, I hope," Grandpa replied as he slammed the door in the chief's face.

Grandpa wrote to senators and representatives, newspapers and radio stations. Finally, in August, he wrote to President Roosevelt.

Unfortunately, before there could be a response, Betty-Dean distracted the town once more. One night she began screaming in her cell. Nothing, no one, could quiet her. A doctor was called. Betty-Dean bit him and went on screaming. She was trussed up in a straitjacket and taken by ambulance to the county hospital in Seattle. The following afternoon she simply walked away, wearing a coat belonging to a nurse. Two nights later, she reappeared in Rider's Dock, with another shotgun.

Within an hour, she shot out the windows in her dead husband's favorite saloon. She went immediately to Pastor Woodie's church, where she blew off the door. Then she ran to her lawyer's house, where she blasted the windshield of his car. And then she walked to the police station, fired her last two shots into Pete's door, and disappeared into the night, smiling. It was reported that she said she hated loose ends.

"Judas Priest," Grandpa howled when he learned about Betty-Dean's rampage. "She could have waited until we got Rider back."

If Chief Carmichael ever heard from President Roosevelt, he didn't tell us. He had a lot on his mind.

I watched Grandpa's futile efforts to interest someone in Rider's disappearance, and I wondered at his persistence. And I wondered why he couldn't see how hopelessly he loved the promises held out by men's laws. He was like someone who refused to believe that his best-beloved had no heart.

"Letters won't do any good," I told him. "Nobody helps because nobody really cares about Rider."

"They've got to care," he said. "This isn't one of those dangbusted foreign countries where only the rich are protected by the laws. Stealing Rider was a crime. Whoever took him has got to be caught, and Rider has to be given back to us."

After that Grandpa began provoking Pastor Woodie. He stopped him in the street whenever he saw him, to accuse and argue and denounce. He marched into the church in the middle of a Sunday service and demanded to know the names of the men who came to take Rider away.

Mama and I learned of this because Deacon Arbuthnot called Chief Carmichael and had him go to the church to take Grandpa home.

I knew, then, that Grandpa had gone too far. Pastor Woodie would take revenge on us, one way or another.

I had no confidant in those days except Druid Annie, and when I slipped away to visit her that afternoon, she wasn't there. I turned away from her house, swallowing hard against the knot of fear that choked me. Instead of going home, I walked down through the town to the waterfront and turned south toward the old dock where steamers had once loaded and unloaded goods for our small farming community.

Wind drove waves against the sea wall. Far out on the sound, a freighter plowed south toward Seattle. During the summer before, Grandpa had taken us here for a picnic. The tide had been out and we'd climbed down the sea wall

74

and spread our blankets on the sand on the sheltered side of a pile of driftwood. I'd built Rider a sand castle, and he and Jonah had collected clam shells to reinforce the castle walls. Druid Annie and Grandpa had bickered about whether or not seaweed was safe to eat, while Mama toasted hot dogs over the fire that Hank built.

Rider. He'd been gone almost two months. Every morning I woke certain that that was the day we'd get him back. Every night I prayed that the ones who took him would realize that he would never love them as he had loved us and so bring him home.

Every day I looked for him down every street I crossed. He'd be a little taller now — he grew so fast. He'd know more words.

And each day he was gone, he'd forget a little more about us.

Above me, sea gulls called mournfully. Through a dazzle of tears, I watched them ride the wind. For the first time, I admitted to myself that we might never see Rider again.

The next day two social workers from the county came to investigate us. They arrived in the late afternoon, before Mama came home from work.

Grandpa answered their knock, listened while they introduced themselves, and then said, "You can't come in." He slammed the door in their faces.

The tall one, Miss Branch, knocked again, glaring at us through the glass.

"You'd better let us in, Mr. Chance," she called out. "It's in your own best interests to cooperate with us. At least it is if you want to keep those children."

"Let them in," I pleaded with Grandpa. "If we make

them mad, they might do something awful." I was so frightened that my hands shook. Pastor Woodie was responsible for this disaster. I'd heard a dozen horror stories from Hank about the county social workers. If a bad situation could possibly be made worse, those women would know the way.

Grandpa opened the door and stepped aside. Miss Branch and Miss Meedly marched inside and looked around the living room before sitting down, uninvited, side by side on the sofa.

They were ugly women, one too thin and the other too fat. They wore nearly identical gray dresses, and I noticed with fascination that Miss Branch had remarkably hairy legs. She even had a wiry, dark mustache.

Jonah, who'd been sitting near the stove in Mama's rocker, got up quietly and crept upstairs.

Miss Branch looked after him. "Is that the retarded boy?"

Grandpa glared, unblinking, at her.

"Yes," I said. "That's Jonah. I'm Rachel."

Miss Branch wrote something down in a little green book. Miss Meedly took out a book just like it from her big black purse.

"What do you want?" I asked.

Miss Meedly studied me carefully, taking note of my overalls and boots. "Do you go to school?" she asked.

"Yes," I said. "I'll be in the tenth grade in September."

"Do you go to school in those clothes?" she asked.

My face burned. "I've been working in the barn. I can't wear a dress there."

Hank chose that moment to burst in the kitchen door, shouting for me before he knew we had enemies among us.

"Rachel!" he bawled. "Get out here. You said you'd be right back."

He stopped in the doorway and stared.

Miss Meedly stared back. "Who is this?" she asked.

I explained that Hank was our hired helper.

"Mr. Chance," Miss Meedly said, "do you let this girl spend much time in the barn with the hired man?"

Hank turned and left, banging the kitchen door behind him.

"Judas Priest," Grandpa cried, "what the hell is that supposed to mean?"

Miss Meedly waited, her pencil poised over her book.

Out in the driveway, an ancient sedan pulled up behind the social workers' car, and any hope I'd had that this afternoon could be saved just died. Through the window, I saw Mama getting out of the passenger seat, helped by Sam Washington. Sam often drove Mama home during those last weeks.

Now he took a sack of groceries out of the back seat and carried it to the porch for Mama, then returned to his car. Miss Branch and Miss Meedly looked at each other and then at the door.

Mama came in, and I saw that she was steeled for the worst.

"These women are from the county," Grandpa said.

Mama put down the grocery sack. "I see," she said. She was pale, but she held her head high. "Why are you here?"

I saw how Miss Meedly's mean eyes raked over Mama, and I read her mind. Miss Meedly would hate any pretty woman, but Mama wasn't just pretty. She was also a breaker of rules. She'd had a baby when she wasn't married. She rode in the front seat of a colored man's car, instead of sitting in back, pretending that he was her driver.

"We've been asked to determine whether or not this is a suitable home for a young girl," Miss Meedly said.

Something flickered behind Mama's eyes. I thought of a bird I'd once rescued that had been tangled in a string. "Who said that this is not a suitable home for Rachel?" Mama said.

Miss Branch smiled coyly. "We can't tell you that."

"Woodie," Grandpa said. He snorted.

"Rachel," Mama said quietly, "will you please excuse us?"

"You want me to leave?" I asked. "But I want to stay. They're going to talk about me, and I want to hear it."

"Rachel, please."

I left the house and stumbled toward the barn. Hank must have been watching, because he opened the door for me.

"I finished the work," he said.

"Then go home."

He sat down on a stool. "I'll go when Abel tells me to go."

I turned my back on him and sighed. "The county's going to take me away from here."

"No," Hank said. "Not yet. They're just trying to scare Abel. They don't want to take kids if they don't have to."

I looked over my shoulder at him. "You don't believe that."

"The Websters are experts," he said sourly. "Trust me. The women like to meddle, but the county doesn't have enough money to take a kid away from every family they pester. Things have to be pretty bad."

78

"Things are pretty bad," I said.

Hank was silent for a moment. "Well," he said slowly, reluctantly, "it didn't help that your mama didn't marry Rider's father. The women from the county don't like stuff like that."

"Well, who does!" I cried. "Do you think Mama wanted things to be this way? Rider's father doesn't have a job. He doesn't even know about Rider! He writes Mama letters, but he never stays anyplace very long, and Mama doesn't want to make him feel bad." Before I'd finished speaking, I knew that I'd blurted out Mama's secret.

"She doesn't want him to feel bad!" Hank shouted. "Is she crazy? Rider was stolen! Maybe the guy could help."

"How?" I said. "What could he do? If Grandpa can't convince anybody to care about what happened, how much good do you think a fruit picker can do?" I rubbed my eyes to stop tears from forming. "If something like this had happened to another family, one that had money, one where the parents . . ."

"Yeah," Hank said, understanding me perfectly.

"Well, then," I went on doggedly, "things would have been different. But nobody thought Mama should keep Rider anyway. Now they all think that he's better off wherever he is."

"With Billy Bong's people?"

"Do you believe that's where Rider is?" I'd never dared ask him the question before. "Chief Carmichael said they don't have him. He had the police in lots of places checking. He thinks we're crazy."

"I know," Hank said. "He tells everybody that."

I bit my lip. "What else does he say behind our backs?"

79

Hank looked straight at me. "He says that Rider probably wandered away and died."

I clenched my fists. "I'll never believe that."

"Most people don't. Most people think Billy Bong's people took him and it was for Rider's own good."

"And what do you think?" I asked Hank straight out.

Hank was quiet for a long time. Then he said, "I think that this is a rotten world and bad things happen all the time. I think that if we care about something, or someone, we'll only end up getting hurt. I think that we can't ever win."

I jumped to my feet, enraged. "How can you say that? What's wrong with you?" I wanted to hit him and knock him down. "You coward!" I shouted. "You're even worse than Grandpa and Mama! He thinks the law is going to help us! Mama thinks that begging is going to get Rider back. But you, you're the dumbest one of all! You gave up!"

I ran out of the barn. Hank was every bit as thick and stupid as I'd ever believed he was and I promised myself never to repeat my mistake of confiding in him.

When I reached the house, I found that the women were gone. Mama, white and trembling, had started dinner, and Grandpa was pulling on his boots, preparing to go out to the barn.

"What happened?" I asked him.

"They're bluffing," he said. "Don't worry." He limped toward the door.

"Grandpa." When he glanced back at me, I said, "Don't write any more letters."

He slammed the door behind him.

I ran up to my room to change out of my overalls. Jonah's door was closed and he was silent behind it.

There was a picture of Rider in a round wood frame on my dresser. I picked it up and looked at him.

"Rider," I said aloud, "I'm going to find you and take you back. Sis is coming, Rider. Don't be scared anymore."

✥ Eight

Cousin Samantha Devereaux and her husband lost the farm to the bank and came to stay with us.

The old house had two bedrooms downstairs, Grandpa's and the one Rider had shared with Mama. There were two small rooms in the attic, mine and Jonah's. Neither had space for much more than a single bed and a small dresser.

"I'll give them my room and sleep on the sofa," Mama volunteered. "When Rider comes back, we'll work out something."

There was a devastating moment of silence.

"They'll take my room," Grandpa grumbled. "I'll sleep on the cot in the barn storeroom."

"But it's cold at night," Samantha protested.

By way of answer, Grandpa pulled spare blankets out of the hall closet and stomped off into the dark.

No one used the little room in one corner of the barn. Hank had been invited to move in there, but so far he had escaped the necessity of leaving home. When Grandpa shoved open the door to the room that evening, it would

82

be for the first time in many months. I didn't envy him the cobwebs and dust.

He came back in a few minutes and tossed the blankets over a chair. "You're right," he said. He had an odd look about him. "It's cold as a mermaid's heart out there. I'll sleep on the sofa." He glared at Mama and me, as if inviting an argument.

"I can sleep in the barn, Grandpa," I said.

"You stay out of there," he growled. "I mean it."

During the same week that Cousin Samantha and Jacob came, Betty-Dean stormed the town again. Everyone had assumed that she'd left Rider's Dock after taking revenge on the men who had betrayed her in one way or another. But if she had left, she came back. She still had the shotgun.

Pastor Woodie had only recently invested a large amount of money in a big billboard on the highway. Each week the message changed. First it read, "The Devil Loves a Stingy Giver."

"Woodie must want a new car," Grandpa had responded.

Next the message read, "The Devil Loves a Disobedient Wife."

Someone else responded to that, and blew two holes in the billboard in the middle of the night.

"I suppose it was Betty-Dean who ruined Pastor Woodie's billboard," I said to Hank the next afternoon as we pulled weeds in the garden.

He sat back on his heels, scowling. "Why does it have to be my aunt? Half the people in town hate that sign."

I grinned. "Half the people in town are women, and I'll bet most of them didn't blame Betty-Dean for anything."

Hank went back to work, his back to me. "Neither do I," he muttered.

"But she killed your uncle."

"No loss," Hank said flatly.

I stood up and wiped my hands on my overalls. "I'm going in the house for a glass of milk. You want some?"

"After I finish up," he said. "You always leave everything half done."

"I do not!" I cried, but then, reluctantly, I decided that he wasn't worth the argument. I'd lost my taste for bickering with him after Rider was stolen. There was no joy in anything.

In the kitchen, I poured myself a glass of milk and opened the breadbox to take out the roll I'd saved for an afternoon snack. It was gone.

Jonah came in, silent as he always was those days, and he put a half-full egg basket on the table.

"Jonah, darn it, did you take the roll I was saving?"

He shook his head.

Then Grandpa must have taken it. "I'm hungry," I said, more to myself than to Jonah, and I pulled open the icebox door. Almost empty. Six people went through a lot of food.

"Did Grandpa and the cousins go into town?" I asked Jonah.

He nodded.

"I sure hope they stop by Patterson's store."

Jonah nodded.

I gave him a long look, thinking of the half-full basket of eggs. "You look funny, as if you've been up to something. Have you been feeding Banjo raw eggs again?"

He shook his head solemnly, but he backed away.

"Then what?"

He turned and ran out the kitchen door, and scuttled across the yard toward the barn. Banjo loped after him, tongue out. They disappeared inside.

I'd check later, I thought, but I forgot until the next day, when everyone in town was talking about how someone had thrown eggs against the windows of the saloon.

Jonah? I thought, and then dismissed the idea immediately. Our grief was making me crazy. I had to do something to end our agony. One way or another. And I had a secret I couldn't bear alone any longer. I'd discovered that Mama had been writing letters, too.

One Saturday morning, I sneaked away to Druid Annie's house. She was brewing a concoction on the stove, and her kitchen smelled of camomile. "Sit down and help yourself to some of Millie's nice brown bread," she said when she let me in.

I cut a slice of bread and spread apple butter on it. "How's Millie doing?" I asked, making nervous conversation. I'd come for a reason, but I was beginning to doubt myself.

Annie poured her remedy into a thick pottery jar, dropped in three ugly dried leaves, and then capped it with a heavy lid. "She only stayed a minute or two. She was on her way to an Altar Guild meeting. They're getting ready for the church fair."

Annie sat across from me and cut herself a slice of bread. "What brings you here this morning with that funny expression on your face. Are you up to some sort of mischief?"

I swallowed the bread in my mouth. "Not yet," I told her.

She sighed and settled herself comfortably. "Tell me."

"Where is Billy Bong now?"

Annie had small, dark brown eyes, and usually they were like a teddy bear's, bright and innocent. But sometimes she had a way of looking straight inside my head, and she'd pick through my thoughts and decide which ones needed exploring.

"Don't go after Billy Bong," she said. "Forget that idea."

I looked back, straight at her, and I offered for her silent examination my grief and my anger with the ways of the adult world. There was no integrity in that world, no true sense of right and wrong. The games that were played would sicken a thieving jaybird.

"Ah, Rachel," she said, sighing.

"I am going after Billy Bong," I said. "He knows where Rider is, and I'm finding my brother and bringing him back home. After that, everybody can argue about who's important enough to bother with and who's got the right to decide. That's the *grown-up* way. They're all too old and scared to see how stupid it is."

She blinked and looked down at her fat little hands. "I can't decide whether to be flattered or insulted that you said that to me. Does Abel know what you're up to?"

"Not yet," I said. "I need you to talk him into helping."

She looked up at me quickly. "Talk him into what?"

"Driving me. I can't do it unless someone drives me there, wherever Rider is, and back again. Hitchhiking won't work. It would be too hard with a little kid. And the people who've got Rider might try to stop me. Grandpa has to drive me. I'll do everything else, once I find out where Billy Bong is going next. I know he knows where Rider is. I *know*."

"You're talking about stealing Rider back," Annie said. She smiled. "I like that idea."

"You can see that it's the right thing to do."

She nodded. "Oh, it's the right thing, Rachel. Just finding him wouldn't be enough. By the time all the police and lawyers and everybody else get through bumbling around, Rider'll be old enough to vote."

"That's what I figured," I said.

"Abel means well," Annie said suddenly, defensively.

"I know."

"He thinks that if he's honorable, he'll be repaid in kind. Then he goes into a rage when things don't work out that way. I've heard him say that if you don't want trouble with rats you have to think like a cat. But he still leaves his cheese on a shelf and puts the cat outside for the night, just because it's his right."

"I know that, too."

Annie sighed again. "I always did believe that Rider was still alive, no matter what they say downtown. And I always believed that Pastor Woodie and Billy Bong knew everything there is to know about what happened that day. But I never could think of how to discover what they know. What are you going to do when you find Billy Bong?"

I cut myself another piece of bread, not because I was hungry but because I needed something to do with my hands. "Watch for his sister, Pearl Sweet."

Annie sucked in her breath. "Yes."

"I never forgot how she looked at Rider that day she rode past us in the car. And how she looked at other little kids the night Hank and I went to the revival meeting."

"But you told all that to Chief Carmichael, and he said you had too much imagination."

"Sure," I said and then I added, "He's made a choice. He'd rather look for Betty-Dean. That's easier and it makes the men in town happier."

"You know that Billy Bong and Pearl could be a long way away. Maybe they're still in California."

"I don't care where they are," I said. "I've got to do something. Things are so awful at home. It gets worse all the time. Mama's been writing letters to Pearl."

Annie leaned forward. "I hadn't heard that."

"She doesn't know that I know. Once I came downstairs in the middle of the night for a glass of water. Mama was in the bathroom. The letter she was writing was on the kitchen table." I swallowed hard. "She wrote, 'I beg you to tell me if my son is still alive.' She sent it to Pearl in care of Pastor Woodie. That letter came back marked 'Refused,' just like a dozen others. She keeps them in a shoe box under her bed."

Annie pulled a folded handkerchief from her apron pocket and dabbed at her eyes. "Did you tell Abel?"

I shook my head. "He must know. He picks up the mail."

Annie raised her gaze to the window behind me and blinked a couple of times. "I'll find out where the Anointed Children are. I'll ask Millie to help. Some of the people from Father Gates's church go out of town to the revivals. Millie will know who to ask."

I nodded. "I'll go wherever they are. And when Pearl Sweet shows up, I'll be waiting."

"What will you do?"

I slumped in the chair. "I don't know yet. Whatever works, I guess. If Rider's with her, I'll just grab him and run. If he isn't, then I guess we'll have to follow her until we find out where she's keeping him."

"What if she doesn't bring him along? What if she leaves him behind somewhere?"

The "what if's" had been keeping me company night after night. I sat up straight. My fists were clenched so hard that my hands hurt.

"I'm going to get my brother back," I said. "Mama's going crazy and Grandpa is sick all the time and Jonah — he doesn't talk or sing. He sits in his bedroom looking out the window day after day. And Rider is growing older. Maybe he won't remember us much longer. That's why I have to find Pearl Sweet now."

It took Annie and Millie two long days to learn where Billy Bong would be crusading for souls that August. I stopped at Annie's house several times a day, and finally Millie was there, waiting for me. She thrust a printed announcement into my hand.

"It came to the church this morning," she said. "Father Gates's secretary remembered that I'd been asking around for information on the revival and she gave me this."

It was a list of places and dates for appearances of "Dr. W. H. Bong, pastor of the internationally acclaimed Tabernacle of Holy Enlightenment."

I read it quickly, and then again, slowly. "He's going through Eastern Washington in August, and then to

Idaho." I looked up at Annie. "Look what it says on the bottom of the page."

She took it from me and read the last line. "'Dr. Bong will be accompanied by the Tabernacle Angels, featuring Pearl Sweet and the Paradise Trio.'" Annie made a wry face. "If this situation weren't so serious, I'd laugh."

"I wish you'd tell me what the two of you wanted with this list," Millie complained. "I've got a feeling you're up to something that might get you in terrible trouble."

Annie folded the list and tucked it in her pocket. "Don't ask and I won't have to lie to you," she told Millie. "Just trust me that it's important."

"It's about Rider, isn't it?" Millie said, and her eyes filled with sympathetic tears. "You found out for sure that one of those Anointed Children stole him."

Annie put her finger to her lips. "Don't even think about it. If Pastor Woodie — "

"I'd rather die than let him find out anything," Millie said abruptly. She reached out and hugged Annie hard. "I don't know what you're going to do, but if I can help, tell me."

After she left, Annie gave me the paper. "It's best that she doesn't know what you have in mind yet. If Abel does agree to go, when will you leave? What will you tell your mama?"

"We'll go so that we show up at the same place and time that Billy Bong does. As for telling Mama, well, that's the tricky part. I don't want her to go with us."

"But why not? She's Rider's mother."

"She's not tough enough. Sometimes I wonder if she's not half out of her mind. We'll have to find a way to convince her that she'll do the most good by staying behind."

"Abel's likely to want to call on the law to help out, you know," Annie warned. "He'll want revenge."

"He won't, because we're going to convince him that the only way to do it is to steal Rider from those people, just like they stole him from us, and then run. And I'm not going to tell Mama anything until just before we leave."

Annie played with crumbs on the table, not looking at me. "You're awfully young for all this, Rachel."

"In my history book at school, I read about a king who led an army when he was my age. I guess I can bring one little boy home."

Annie sighed. "Maybe you won't have to go that far. Who knows what might happen before you go."

I tightened my lips. "Nothing ever happens that we don't make happen."

❧ Nine

Cousin Jacob was a quiet, kind man, grieving for his lost farm, but he worked hard on Grandpa's land and there was very little for Hank to do anymore. Grandpa didn't want to fire Hank, so he gave him what work he could and Hank didn't complain.

In fact, Hank came even when there was no work for him to do. He hung around the barn, or sometimes just sat on the fence and watched summer ripen. We rarely spoke, even though I was spending more time outdoors. In the house, my work was done by Cousin Samantha, in spite of her bad hip.

On Sunday morning, I pulled myself up on the fence beside Hank. "How come you're always here, even when there isn't much for you to do?" I asked.

He gave me a long-suffering look but didn't answer. He didn't need to. I suspected that he was avoiding his family.

Millie had told Annie, who told all of us, that Hank's mother was speaking out in public for Betty-Dean. She and some of the other women in Rider's Dock decided that Betty-Dean had killed her husband in self-defense. No one was able, yet, to think of an excuse for her coming back and shooting up the town, though, but they were working on it. Hank's father didn't like anyone siding with the woman who had murdered his brother, so he gave his wife a sample of what Betty-Dean had suffered at the hands of Mike. Or so Millie had reported.

Hank and I sat without speaking for five minutes, watching a black hen and her six half-grown chicks.

"Why do you always bring food with you when you come?" I asked him. He'd arrived that morning with an enormous lunch packed in a grocery sack. "We've always fed you."

"You've got enough people to feed." Abruptly, he jumped down.

"Where are you going?"

Without looking at me, he said, "Into town. Maybe John Patterson needs some help cleaning the store." He loped off and didn't trouble himself with saying goodbye.

I saw Jonah slip into the barn, with Banjo right behind. Cousin Jacob was working inside and would be glad for Jonah's silent company. I wandered back to the house in time for a mid-morning cup of coffee with Cousin Samantha and Grandpa.

But just as we sat down, Druid Annie trotted through the open doorway, panting a little. She seemed surprised to see all of us in the kitchen.

"Come in, old girl, and have a cup of java," Grandpa said. Samantha rushed to get another cup and echoed Grandpa's invitation.

Annie looked distractedly around. "I thought I'd be able to catch you outside, Abel," she said.

"Well, you caught me inside," he said. "What's the poop, Annie?"

She scowled, momentarily distracted from her errand. "Isn't he awful, Samantha? We've got to apologize for that mouth of his."

Cousin Samantha smiled tolerantly. "All the Chance men have mouths that won't quit." She filled a cup for Annie but didn't sit back down with us. "Excuse me, Annie. I've got beds to make and I don't know what all. You sit and rest."

Samantha gave me a look, but I pretended I didn't understand and propped my elbows on the table, waiting. So this was the time Annie had chosen to tell Grandpa about my plan. No wonder she looked agitated. Anything could happen.

"Abel, I heard that John Patterson made you an offer for your truck," she said. "Don't you sell it to him."

I gaped at her, then at Grandpa. "You can't sell the truck!"

"Jacob's is newer than mine and runs better. We don't need two trucks here, and we do need some extra cash. The barn has to be reroofed before the fall rains start."

"You can't sell the truck!" I cried, seeing my plans to steal Rider disintegrating before the onslaught of another Chance family financial crisis.

"You're going to need your truck," Annie began.

"If I need one, I'll use Jacob's," Grandpa howled. "Judas H. Priest, what's wrong with the two of you?"

"You can't involve Jacob in what's going to be happening when you and Rachel go after Billy Bong," Annie cried.

That shut up Grandpa so successfully that for a moment

94

I thought he'd quit breathing. He leaned over the table at Annie. "What the hell are you talking about?"

Annie's gaze flickered over me and then steadied on Grandpa. She told him about the list and what I wanted to do.

His face grew redder and redder while he listened. When she finished, he turned to me. "You're going to steal Rider? You worked out all these dingbusted plans? You're taking over my goddam truck and ordering me around? I think you better leave plans and plots to the grown-ups around here."

I clenched my fists. My anger mixed with panic. "No!" I shouted. "I'm going to steal Rider back because I'm sick of waiting for somebody to pay attention to your letters and I'm sick of Mama begging and pleading and crying. Nobody is going to help us except us! I know Pearl Sweet's got Rider. I *know*. I saw how she looked at him."

Grandpa opened his mouth to speak.

"Now, Abel . . ." Annie began, and she reached across the table and put her hand on his arm.

He shook off her hand. "Quit your pawing, Annie. Rachel, goddammit, we don't know for sure who's got Rider. Maybe one of those other lying, thieving lunatics has him —"

"It's Pearl Sweet, Abel," Annie cried, anguished. "It's Pearl Sweet who's got Rider because she can't have babies of her own."

Grandpa sucked in his breath. "Old lady, you'd better be sure of that. Pete Carmichael already said she doesn't have him."

"Rachel and I are sure," she said. "Pete only took somebody else's word for it. If Rachel says that's where Rider is, then that's where he is. She's so close to him that she can see true about him, and this morning I saw it in the tea leaves."

"Tea leaves!" bawled Grandpa. "The tea leaves told you that Pearl Sweet has Rider?"

Druid Annie banged her hand on the table. "Yessir!" she shouted.

Grandpa took out his handkerchief and blew his nose explosively. I girded myself with what was left of my courage, and I saw Annie clasp her hands together. If he smiled his terrible smile now, we were finished.

"All right, then," Grandpa said in his normal tone of voice. He got up for his whiskey bottle and slopped some into his coffee while Annie and I sat in stunned silence. "Women," he muttered, and he took a deep swallow from his cup. "Why didn't you give me more notice? That blasted junk pile of a truck needs a good tune-up and a little work on the clutch." He peered at Annie from under his eyebrows. "When did you say Billy Bong gets to . . . where was it? Soap Lake?"

She took a breath. "He'll be there in two days."

Grandpa blinked. "Why, then so will we," he said.

I grinned. "Okay. And you know Mama's not well enough, or tough enough, to go with us. What are we going to tell her?"

"To stay here and pray," Grandpa said. "She'll see the sense of it. If she doesn't, then I'll remind her how much we need the money she brings in. She'd lose that job if she took off."

I hoped he was right, but in the end it was Jacob who wanted to go, leaving me behind where I'd be "safe." He argued fiercely with Grandpa for most of the afternoon before we left. Grandpa silenced Jacob finally by banging his fist on the table and saying, "Rachel goes. It's her plan, so she goes."

That evening we told Mama. She listened in silence, then nodded once. After she went to her room, we could hear her crying for a long time. I was certain that she knew the real reason we didn't want her to go with us, and she was ashamed.

We'd all been in bed for an hour when someone began pounding on the front door. Grandpa answered, and I leaped up and listened at the head of the stairs while Hank's father demanded that Grandpa tell him where Hank was or face the consequences.

"He didn't show up today," Grandpa said. "And I'll thank you, goddammit, to keep your voice down. I've got a houseful of women and children who don't need you scaring the sense out of them."

"He always comes here," Mr. Webster argued. I crept down the stairs and saw him in the doorway, with a small cut under his eye, facing Grandpa belligerently.

Grandpa hiked up the bottoms of his pajamas. "Hank hasn't been around," he said. I was astonished at his reasonable tone. It was fake, of course. But I wondered why he bothered, since he had no use for Hank's drunken and abusive father. "Actually," he went on, "there's no work for Hank since our cousins came to stay."

"Then where is he? You tell me that."

Grandpa took hold of the edge of the door and began easing it closed. "I couldn't tell you. Haven't seen the boy."

Hank's father slammed the door open again. "He's in your barn, isn't he?"

Grandpa exploded. "No, he's not in my barn. There's nothing in my barn but the cows and that dingbusted hen with the bad leg."

"I'm going to have a look for myself," Mr. Webster said.

"And I'll go out with you with my shotgun," Grandpa roared. "If Hank's not there, I'll feel free to blow your goddam butt clear to Mukilteo. Agreed?" He looked back and saw me hugging the wall. "Rachel, fetch my shotgun and be sure it's loaded before you bring it out here."

His bedroom door opened and Jacob stepped out, carrying Grandpa's gun. "You got trouble, Abel?" he asked loudly. "You want me to drive into town for Pete Carmichael?"

Pete Carmichael's name must have conjured up unpleasant memories for Mr. Webster, because he backed out the door. "Hank's run away, then," he said. "I aim to get him back. He's got a few things to answer for."

Grandpa slammed the door. After Mr. Webster's car roared off, Grandpa rubbed his hands through his hair. "By jumping Judas," he said, "you nearly scared me to death, Jacob. Pete Carmichael's exactly what we don't need around here right now."

"No fear, Abel. I was only trying out the idea to see how that man took to it."

Grandpa burst out laughing. "That man's got all the trouble he can handle already," he said. But then he sobered. "Where is Hank? I was so dang busy today I didn't really pay attention. It's not like him to not even drop by."

"Does he know you're leaving tomorrow morning?" Jacob asked.

Grandpa shook his head. "Nobody knows except Annie and Millie. After we're gone, Lara will tell folks that I took Rachel to the ocean to visit Cousin Alma in Hoquiam before school starts."

Jacob nodded briskly. "Good. But if Hank shows up tomorrow, do you want us to tell him that, too?"

"You'd better, just in case," Grandpa said.

"Hank would never tell anybody where we're going," I said to him. "He hates everybody in town just as much as you do."

Grandpa glared at me, but Jacob laughed, then said, "He's right, though, Rachel. The fewer people know, the better chance you have of surprising Billy Bong."

Mama came out, then, pale and fretful. "I was listening. I'm not sure this is the right thing to do. What if you get caught, Abel? I can't bear to lose my daughter, too."

"Mama, that won't happen. How can it be wrong for me to take back the brother who was stolen from us?" I asked.

"It doesn't seem to matter what's right," she said. "The only thing that matters is what people can get away with."

I nodded emphatically. "And you just watch what Grandpa and I are going to get away with."

"Amen to that," Cousin Samantha said from the doorway to her bedroom. "Jacob, come back to bed. If they're going to start at five, we'd better get as much sleep as we can."

We all went back to bed, and for a little while my worries about the quest Grandpa and I were about to undertake were set aside while I worried about Hank. It was obvious that he'd run away at last, and I wondered about the cut on his father's face. Could Hank have been responsible for that? Life was hard and violent in that awful family. Maybe he'd be better off if he got away and stayed there.

But maybe he hadn't left town after all. Maybe he really was in the barn. On a sudden impulse, I leaped out of bed, pulled on a sweater over my nightgown, and tiptoed down the stairs. Only Banjo heard me, and he followed me outside, across the yard, and into the small door on the side of the barn.

The dark smelled of cows and hay. Barefoot, I crept between the stalls, and a startled cow moved heavily, grunting in protest.

The storeroom door was ajar slightly. I pushed it open farther and it creaked.

Someone gasped in the dark.

"Hank?" I asked softly. "Sorry I scared you."

Silence.

It wasn't Hank. Suddenly I knew that with certainty. But it wasn't a stranger, because Banjo pushed past me, his tail flopping against my leg, and greeted the person who lay on the narrow cot.

It was too dark for me to see, and in spite of Banjo's trust, I was too cautious to step inside. "Who is it?" I demanded.

"Rachel, it's Betty-Dean Webster."

I sagged with relief. "I was afraid it was a tramp Banjo had taken up with," I said. I didn't tell her that I believed that she was probably more dangerous.

A match struck and she lit a candle. I saw her then,

thinner than ever. Banjo sat at the foot of her cot watching me.

"I suppose Grandpa knows you're here," I said flatly. "And Cousin Jacob, too, since he's out here so much."

She nodded.

"Does Mama know?"

"No. Your Grandpa was afraid of worrying her even more. But Samantha and Jonah know. And Hank. He brought me here."

"Hank," I said. I remembered the sacks of food. And then I remembered that Hank had disappeared. "He's run away, his dad says. Do you know where he is?"

She sat forward anxiously. "No. He's run off? I don't blame him." She swung her legs off the cot, and I saw that they were bird-thin, and one of her ankles bore hideous old bruises, shading from purple to yellow. "I hope he's all right."

"How long are you going to stay here?" I asked. I was thinking that when I brought Rider back (I didn't dare think *if* I brought him back), it wouldn't do for the Chance family to be harboring a murderer. The women from the county would then be the least of our worries.

"I'll leave as soon as my ankle heals," she said. "I fell and sprained it and I could hardly walk." She looked up at me. "I'll be leaving in another couple of days."

I knew I should offer to take her with us out of town, but I wouldn't do it. If anyone saw her in the truck, we'd be stopped. Rider would slip even further away. I felt guilty, but I had to make a choice. Obviously Grandpa had made the same one, because she didn't seem to know that we were leaving the following morning.

She misread my guilty expression. "Don't be afraid of me."

"I'm not," I said, surprised that this was the truth. She looked more victim than murderer. "But I'm afraid of what will happen if you're found here."

She began to speak, but she gasped instead and leaned forward, gripping her stomach.

"What's wrong?" I asked.

I had to wait a long time for an answer. At last the spasm of pain let go of her and she looked up. "I've got cancer, Rachel. I'm going to die."

"But — "

She raised one hand to protest my interruption. "I only wanted to die in peace, but Mike wouldn't have it." She smiled, but her eyes filled with tears that she wiped hastily.

I cleared my throat. "Well, this is some kind of world," I said. I didn't even try to brush away my own tears. "I don't understand anything. My brother's been stolen because people didn't think that we were good enough for him. The laws my grandpa loves are some kind of terrible joke, because people can choose to follow them or not, and there's nothing anybody can do. At least, there's nothing people like us can do. And you . . . " My nose was running and I pulled a hanky from my sweater pocket.

"But spring still comes every year, Rachel," she said. "And bluebells bloom in the woods, and doves build nests in the trees."

"What difference does that make?" I cried.

"It makes all the difference."

We were silent together for a while in the flickering candlelight. At last I sighed.

"I wish you luck, then," I said, and I turned to go.

"If you hear anything about Hank, will you tell me?"

"If you're still here," I said. I called Banjo and pushed the door closed behind us. It bounced back open an inch or two, and I saw the light from the candle go out.

I wasn't certain how soon we'd be back with Rider, but poor Betty-Dean had to be gone by then. I couldn't blame her for what she'd done to her husband, but if it came to a choice between her or the Chance family, then I'd have to stick with my own blood.

"Forgive me if I'm selfish," I whispered to God, if He was listening. "I'm doing the best I can with what you gave me."

I included a quick prayer for Hank's safety, even though it was remotely possible, I supposed bitterly, that he'd taken shelter with Maysie Clarence.

Ten

Grandpa and Jacob finished loading the truck before five the next morning. The sky was overcast, and the air smelled of dust and summer rain. A thin wind stirred the trees.

"You should take more clothes," Mama said when she looked into the paper sack containing my clean underwear, socks, and an extra sweatshirt like the one I wore under my short jacket.

I shoved the sack under the canvas that covered the truck bed. "I won't need anything but overalls and shirts, Mama."

She pressed her hands against her pale lips for a moment, then sighed and said, "You'll have enough food for four days. That should be enough, don't you think, Abel?"

"Sure," he said. "Plenty."

I wasn't so certain. There was a box of sandwiches and fruit for the first day, along with a big jug of coffee. After that, we'd be using canned goods and crackers, and anything we could buy that was cheap. We barely had enough money for gas.

Jonah sat on the steps beside Banjo, rocking back and forth mournfully. Cousin Samantha slipped her arm around Mama. "Do you have enough blankets, Abel?" she asked.

"We have enough blankets and doodads to outfit the entire British army, dadbust it!" Grandpa cried fretfully, and he aimed a kick at one of the truck tires. He'd listened to an early radio news broadcast that morning and heard that German planes had dropped bombs on England again. Even under ordinary circumstances, this would have angered him. Now he was outraged.

"How did all the lunatics get the upper hand?" he grumbled as he jammed his cap on his head. "Every place I look, madmen are running things. Here, Rachel, quit standing there and gawking. We've got to get moving."

I leaped up on the running board and crawled into the truck cab. I wanted to hug Mama and kiss her, but I was afraid that I'd end up bawling all over her. She was wringing her hands. In another moment, she'd insist on going along. Her anxious, constant suffering would weaken Grandpa and me. "We'll be back soon," I said firmly as I slammed the door.

Grandpa attempted to start the engine, but it barely turned over and then quit with a grunt. "Start, by God, or I'll kick your slats in," he shouted.

"You should take my truck," Jacob said.

"No!" Grandpa thundered. "If you lend me your truck, you'll be involving yourself in whatever comes. Police trouble, maybe. There has to be one man left in this house, no matter what. I'm taking my truck and it's going to start and that's final!" He leaned across me and pulled out the choke knob. The truck started with an ear-splitting roar and a cloud of blue smoke.

Over the racket, I heard Mama say, "Heavens, here's Annie."

There she was, galloping clumsily down the road, carrying a straw suitcase and her knitting bag.

"What do you want?" Grandpa shouted rudely. "We're getting ready to leave."

"I'm going with you," Annie shouted back.

"The hell you say," Grandpa yelled, grabbing the gearshift.

I put my hand over his. "Wait."

Annie dropped her suitcase beside the truck. "I've been thinking it over," she wheezed. "You might need me, so I phoned Millie this morning and told her to take care of my cats and bring Eunice Perry's comfrey tea over to her and — "

"Why don't we all go!" Grandpa cried. "We'll form a caravan. Everybody in town can tag along!"

Annie stuck out her chin. "I'm going, you old sumbitch, so you might as well get out and stow away my suitcase."

"Aw, Judas Priest," Grandpa grumbled. "Rachel, you'll have to ride in back."

Both of us got out, pulled back the canvas and rearranged the provisions to make room for Annie's suitcase and me. I didn't mind. I was in no mood to talk, or to be squeezed in between them. Finally we cleared a corner behind the cab, I made myself comfortable on a folded blanket, and Grandpa climbed back in the driver's seat.

"Can we go now, or should we load up Banjo and one of the cows?" he said. "Or the hen that lays double-yolked eggs?"

Annie slapped his arm. "Go, go." She leaned her head out her window and called to Mama, "We're bringing back your boy, Lara. The cards told me so last night."

"Aw, jumping bejesus," Grandpa snarled, and the truck lurched down the driveway and out to the blacktop road that led to the highway. I pulled a flap of canvas over my legs because the morning was cool, and watched the farm disappear behind us.

Rider, I thought, do you know we're on our way?

We saw only one car on the road out of Rider's Dock. Sam Washington, who worked three nights a week cleaning the Municipal Building, passed us and soberly raised his hat to us.

We drove south along Puget Sound, and then southeast, following a narrow road that traced the tip of Lake Washington. The rain began as we turned toward the mountains at last, chugging determinedly toward Fall City and Sunset Highway, which would take us to Snoqualmie Pass and then Eastern Washington.

I pulled the canvas over my head, and rain pattered busily on it. The sounds of the engine and the wet tires smoothed the sharp edges of my fears of failure. I took Rider's handprint out of my pocket, kissed it, and put it back. Then I dozed.

I woke to the shrill complaint of the truck's brakes and shoved the canvas back so that I could see where we were.

Hank Webster stood beside the country road, wet as a

fish, his dark hair plastered to his forehead. I thought, for a moment, that I was still asleep and struggling through an uneasy dream.

Grandpa's door opened and he shouted, "Judas H. Priest, what are you doing here?"

Hank looked first at Grandpa, then at me peeping out from under the canvas, then back at Grandpa. "I'm going east."

"Well, I sure didn't think you were heading for Alaska," Grandpa said. "Get in the back with Rachel and don't sit on the dadbusted sandwiches."

"Where are you going?" Hank asked.

"East," Grandpa said. Hank nodded.

Begrudgingly, I stood up and folded back the canvas, then set to work with Hank to shift our supplies once more to make room for him and his wet blanket roll. By the time we finished, though, the rain had let up, and so the picture wasn't entirely bleak.

"You can sit across from me," I said, "but make sure you keep your big feet to yourself." We arranged the canvas so that it covered everything but our faces, I reached out and knocked on the cab twice, and the engine roared back to life.

"Truck needs a tune-up," Hank said.

"It beats walking," I snapped. "Especially if you're dumb enough to run away in the rain."

We rode for several minutes in silence, and then Hank pushed the canvas away from his head. "Why are you going east?" he asked.

I glowered at him. "Why do you want to know?"

He glowered back. "I'm on my way to Chicago. How far are you going?"

"Not that far." I settled down and let the canvas droop over my eyes.

"You're going after Rider, aren't you?"

"Nobody knows where Rider is."

Hank snorted. "People could figure it out."

I shoved the canvas back and stared at him. "If that's true, why didn't they help us get him back?"

"Grow up, Rachel. Everybody cares if a rich family's baby is stolen. People like that are like kings and queens, or movie stars. People like the Chances — and the Websters — are different. There are so many of us and we have so much trouble that everybody else gets sick of us. They don't care. Most of the time *we* don't even care."

I bit my lip, but that didn't stop the grief that filled me from spilling out. "I hate you, Hank Webster," I said, and I pulled the canvas over my face.

In that sodden dark, I cried until the knees of my overalls were wet from my tears. I knew Hank spoke the truth, that only a few of us really cared about Rider, that most people had gone to bed that first awful night — thankful that trouble had found the Chance family instead of them. And they gratefully forgot us when Betty-Dean provided them with a spectacular excuse.

Grandpa stopped in Fall City. According to the clock in the gas station window, it was nearly eight o'clock. While the attendant filled the tank, Grandpa and Hank watched gasoline splash inside the glass ball on top of the pump and discussed road conditions and weather. The rain had stopped, but thick clouds hung low over us and the air was saturated.

"There's probably a rest room around back," Annie said to me. "Let's go do our duty, and when we come back, we'll have a swallow or two of coffee. I brought a jugful."

"We've got one, too," I said, thinking that I'd poured out only enough for two when Mama, Samantha, and I had packed the food that morning. Now we were four, and I was glad. Well, not exactly glad about Hank. But Grandpa was relieved, I was certain. He'd have company cursing the truck.

When we finished our coffee, we started up the highway again, passing North Bend in half an hour. Grandpa stopped the car at another gas station and topped off the radiator, although he'd filled it at Fall City.

"What's he doing that for?" I asked Hank.

"We're going to have trouble pretty soon when the radiator starts boiling over."

"But it's not hot today," I said.

"Not yet," Hank said. "We'll climb above the clouds and then it'll be hot enough for you. And you know what happens to the truck then."

Not long after that, the steep road rose above the clouds. Immediately we were under a brilliant, hot sky, and when I looked over the side of the truck, I saw clouds below us then, with the dark tops of fir trees piercing them. The radiator boiled over for the first time about twenty minutes later, and Grandpa stopped.

I jumped out of the truck, peeled off my jacket, and pushed up the sleeves of my sweatshirt. Hank folded the canvas and then took off his wet jacket and shirt.

"I brought a lemon," Druid Annie said as she stood beside the truck, fanning herself with a copy of *Numerology News*. "I could make lemonade if you'll give me some water from those cans, Abel."

"I need every drop for the radiator," Grandpa said, and he kicked the nearest tire.

"Then we'll get water at the next rest stop," Annie said.

"If we make it that far," Grandpa growled, aiming another kick at the tire.

"Keep doing that and you'll boot a hole in the tire before you're done, Abel," Hank said. "It's nearly worn through already."

Grandpa stumped around to the front of the truck and touched the radiator cap gingerly. Steam was still leaking out, but only in fitful hisses now.

"Don't touch that," Annie said, but Grandpa grasped the cap anyway, gave it a quick twist, and pulled it off. Steam gushed out, but then it sputtered and stopped before Grandpa quit shaking his fingers and swearing.

Hank refilled the radiator, using most of our water, and we started off again. The truck's engine labored, and I could have walked as fast as we were moving. We stopped frequently, trying to avoid another boil-over, and once a friendly truck driver pulled up behind us to offer his spare can of water. Grandpa took it and tried to pay the driver for his time and trouble, but the man wouldn't accept the quarter Grandpa held out until Hank insisted. The man tooted his horn as he drove away.

"A quarter for a can of water?" Annie exclaimed. "Are you made of money, old man?"

"He'll have to pay a quarter to buy a new can as big as

this one," Hank said. "Unless he finds one beside the road."

"Nobody finds empty cans along a mountain road," Grandpa said bitterly as he climbed back into the truck. "Not unless you find a car with a gut-shot radiator in the same place."

Shortly after that, the radiator boiled over again, blowing great columns of rusty steam. We had enough water to refill the radiator, but Grandpa was afraid to continue on without carrying water with us. Below, down a steep cliff studded with sharp rocks, a creek crashed noisily along, and so Hank and I scrambled down, with cans tied together with string, then looped around our waists.

The filled cans were heavy. Hank could carry two at once going back up, but I could only manage one, and there were times on the climb up to the road that I was sure I would fall and die on the rocks below.

In spite of the protests of Annie and Grandpa, I went back down with Hank to help with the rest of the cans. Hank didn't say a word, but only grinned at me. I saw sweat on his bare chest, and if I'd dared, I'd have slapped him for being an arrogant caveman.

The heat, my anger, and my determination to show him that I could do what he did, broke my concentration. Halfway down the cliff I slipped. I slid face down, grabbing at anything I could to slow my fall. Once my overalls hung up on a jagged rock, but ripped loose and I tumbled over and over, landing on my back.

I was too stunned to cry out for a moment or two, but by the time Hank reached me, I was beginning to feel pain.

"Are you all right?" Hank bent over me, his face bloodless beneath his dark tan.

I sat up slowly, testing my bones. My hands were cut and one side of my face felt scorched. I touched it gingerly. "Is my cheek bleeding?"

"No, but your knees are," Hank said.

The legs of my overalls were shredded, and my bare, bloody knees stuck through. "I don't have anything else to wear!" I cried, horrified.

"Who cares about your clothes!" Hank shouted. "Are your legs broken or not?"

"Of course they're not broken!" I yelled back, and I got painfully to my feet. "See? See?"

"Are you hurt?" Grandpa called out. "Hank, is she hurt?"

Hank looked at me with such disgust that I stepped back from him. "She's fine," he called to Grandpa. "She's coming up now."

"I'll get a can," I said, hobbling toward the creek.

"No, go back. I'll take the cans." Hank shoved past me. "If you dented one, there'd be less water for the truck."

When I tried to follow him, he turned on me furiously. "You've done enough stupid things for one trip," he said. "Your blood's probably on the rocks. Do you want to attract a cougar? Or a bear? Go back and wait at the truck."

A cougar or a bear? I scrambled back up the cliff. And I hated Hank every foot of the way. I had been bested.

We took a long four hours reaching the summit, with frequent stops to let the radiator cool. Grandpa parked the truck in a rest area near a picnic table shaded by a pine tree, and we piled out, sighing and stretching. I had a thousand separate aches and pains.

"It's all downhill now," Grandpa said. He reached back

in the car, feeling under his seat, and pulled out a small whiskey bottle.

Annie snatched it away. "Oh, no, you don't," she said. "No sir, you're going dry this trip." She tucked the bottle in the pocket of her dress and puttered around to the back of the truck. "Hand me that box, Rachel. Didn't I see sandwiches? And oranges? Oh, good."

Grandpa pulled back his good leg to kick a tire, but he caught Hank's scowl first and spit on the tire instead. "Women," he muttered. "Dingdong it."

We wolfed our food and washed it down with lemonade Annie made, using clear, cold water she got from a nearby drinking fountain.

I'd washed off my wounds, and now they throbbed and stung worse than before. My overalls were beyond mending, although I tried to tack the ragged edges together with thread from Annie's mending kit.

"I don't know what I'm going to do," I told her when I gave up and tucked the mending kit back in her knitting bag.

"We'll have to get you some new clothes when we get to Ellensburg," she said.

"I can't afford new duds," Grandpa interrupted. "I'm sorry, ladies, but I need every cent for the truck."

"Abel, you'd give a quarter to a stranger and begrudge your own kin a dollar or two to cover her nakedness!"

Hank grinned at this. I clenched my fists. "I've got my birthday dollar. If there's a dime store in Ellensburg, I can find something to wear."

Annie, her beady eyes fixed on Grandpa, groped through her knitting bag and pulled out a coin purse. "Save your birthday money, child. I've got plenty." She opened the coin purse a crack and displayed, for our amazement, a roll of paper money.

"What did you do, dig up your family fortune?" Grandpa asked.

"I'm a woman of independent means, Abel. Never mind where I got it." Annie put back her money. "Let's get going. We should be in Soap Lake by six."

We reached Ellensburg by three o'clock, and Grandpa stopped at a gas station across the street from a five-and-dime, where Annie bought me a bright yellow cotton skirt and an orange blouse with puffed sleeves for ninety-eight cents plus three cents tax. I'd never worn anything but drab colors before, but since Annie was paying, I had to let her do the choosing. I changed in the store rest room and dropped my rolled-up overalls in the trash bin.

When Grandpa first saw me, he cleared his throat and said, "You look just like your aunt Althea, bless her soul." Althea was his sister who died of pneumonia when she was sixteen.

But Hank didn't say anything at all. I'd expected him to tease me or ridicule my gaudy finery, and so his uneasy silence was a relief. I was suddenly conscious, for the first time in my fifteen years, that I really, truly, was glad to be a girl.

Would Rider recognize his sister like this? Oh, yes, for we knew each other heart to heart, not just eye to eye.

❧ Eleven

We left Ellensburg at three-thirty, and Billy Bong's revival meeting at Soap Lake was scheduled to begin at six. Grandpa was certain that the worst of the trip was over, so we crossed the Columbia River in great spirits.

But the right rear tire blew out with a bang after we left Vantage. Grandpa pulled off the road into a rest area where a dilapidated old bus was parked. A dozen men rested in its shade, and when they saw us, they got up and strolled lazily over to take turns inspecting the tire and sympathizing with Grandpa.

"It's a goner, friend," one said. He helped Hank pull the spare tire from the slot in the left front fender.

Hank, looking hopeful, bounced the tire and then scowled. "It might only need air."

The man took the tire and bounced it. Several other men gathered around, shaking their heads. "It's close to being flat, friend," the first man told Grandpa. "We'd better have a look-see at the inner tube. If you're lucky, it won't need a patch."

"Gawd Almighty," Grandpa cried, "if it's not one thing it's ten."

The men laughed cheerlessly. They looked as if they knew what it was like to have everything go wrong at once.

The man who spoke first held out his hand to Grandpa. "The name's Casey Shay. We've got some work waiting for us down the road a way, and then we drop over to Yakima to pick up the rest of the crew and head east to Spokane."

Hank's eyes lighted up at the word "east." But Grandpa looked regretful. "Crop chasing, are you? That's hard work."

"Beats no work at all," Casey Shay said. "I've got a good crew here and we've been lucky picking up jobs. It's the long winter I hate to see coming. We'll have to go back to California, and there'll be hundreds more just like us, all looking for work." He nodded at Druid Annie and touched the brim of his hat. "Ma'am," he said. He gave me a big, gap-toothed smile. "How do, miss. My girls are about your age. Twins, named Kathleen and Maureen."

Grandpa introduced Druid Annie, Hank, and me. We shook hands with the men closest to us, and then Hank and Casey set about prying the inner tube out of the tire. It was nearly flat.

"Slow leak, I'll bet," Casey said. "You'll have to take it to a gas station. They'll have a tub of water you can shove the tube in and then you'll see where the bubbles are coming from."

"Where's the nearest station?" Hank asked Casey.

He and his men conferred. Then he told Hank that he

should walk back toward the river. "Might be a mile," he said.

"But we have to be in Soap Lake by six," I said. "We *have* to be there."

Casey shook his head slowly. "I don't think you'll make it, miss." He pushed his hat back and looked up at the sun. "Tell you what, folks. We can spare you some of our time. We'll drive you to the station and bring you back. That'll shave off an hour."

"Then let's go," I said. I didn't dare think what would happen if we didn't get to the revival that night.

The men boarded their bus, and Hank wrestled the tire up the steps. Grandpa handed me a dollar bill folded over twice. "We have to replace that dingbusted blowout, too. Tell Hank to ask the man if he's got a cheap used tire that'll do the job."

"Is this going to be enough?" I fretted as I took the dollar.

Grandpa produced another bill. "Try not to spend it, girl."

"You could ask Annie to lend us some money," I whispered.

"Forget that!" Grandpa growled.

Casey, behind the wheel of the bus, waved at Annie and Grandpa, and the bus started with a broken roar. I sat down in an empty front seat and stared out at the sun-bleached land.

Rider, don't be scared, I thought. We're still coming.

At the gas station, Casey and Hank helped the man repair the tire, but it took time. More than an hour passed before the leak was found and the patch cooled enough so that they could take the inner tube out of the press and test it again for bubbles. Meanwhile, some of the men from the bus sorted through a pile of used tires until they found one that would fit the truck. It took longer to find an inner tube to go inside it. They helped me out with dickering for the price, and at last we loaded two tires on the bus and headed back for the rest area. We got off the bus at fifteen minutes to six.

"Now what are we going to do?" I asked Grandpa after the bus left. "It's too late to get Rider tonight." I was working hard to keep from panicking.

"Billy Bong and his sister will probably be staying in Soap Lake tonight," Grandpa said. "We'll find 'em. And then tomorrow morning, as soon as they stick their heads out of their holes, we'll grab Rider and head home."

He made it sound so simple, so possible. I was tired and hot, and beginning to believe that we were all crazy. We had no real plan for stealing Rider. Until then, I'd been trusting to my instincts. But the truck was acting as if it were an agent of Billy Bong's own design, bent on keeping us away from Rider.

Druid Annie pulled her straw suitcase from the back of the truck. "Get that tire on," she said. "I'll fix us something to eat while you're doing that."

"We'll eat when we get to Soap Lake," Grandpa said.

"But that's three hours away!" Annie complained. "Be sensible, Abel. It'll be dark by the time we get there. Rider will be in bed somewhere."

"She's right, Grandpa," I said reluctantly. "We might as well eat here." I wasn't hungry myself. The lump in my throat was choking the appetite out of me.

Druid Annie's suitcase was like a small storeroom. She

took out a camp stove, two pans, and a coffeepot. And package after package of herbs.

"I knew Lara would send along food," she said. "So I brought medicine."

I lifted a box of canned goods down from the truck. "We won't get sick," I said.

"Your grandpa's leg is getting worse," she said. "And nobody knows what's going to happen next. Or what shape Rider will be in when we get him." This last was said quietly.

My gaze jerked toward her. "They wouldn't hurt him," I said, gasping with a new fright.

"He's been scared out of his wits," she said as she took the can opener out of the box and used it on two cans of beans. "And it's late summer. There are all kinds of things around that a scared little kid might catch. Stomach trouble, for instance. Infections. And this is rattlesnake country." She dumped the beans into a pan and lit the camp stove.

"And it's polio season, too," I said bitterly as I flapped a tablecloth over the nearest picnic table. "Or Rider could have burned himself or broken his leg. You aren't doing much to cheer me up, Annie."

Annie stole a quick look at Grandpa and Hank, working on the truck. "I brought herbs to help Abel if he starts craving whiskey," she said. "I can make a poultice for his leg, too. I can even dress those banged-up knees of yours, girl. They look infected to me. I can help with almost anything that happens, so don't you get sassy with me. The folks that deal best with trouble are the ones who are prepared for it."

Tears of shame stung my eyes. I turned and threw my arms around her. "I'm sorry. But I'm so scared now that I can't feel Rider waiting for me anymore."

"Oh, he's waiting for you," she murmured, patting my back while I wept. "Maybe we missed him tonight, but we've time, all the time we need."

"Did you really see us getting Rider back in the cards?" I asked.

She was silent for a moment. "I saw *you* getting him back, Rachel."

I looked at her through eyes blurred by tears. "I don't understand."

"Neither did I." She blinked unhappily. "Well, it's all half-fake, anyway, the cards and tea leaves. Seeing or dreaming true are different. You know that. How could you get Rider without us being right there with you? Come on, now, let's get food on the table."

We ate quickly, and within an hour we were on the road to Soap Lake. I was surprised that Hank was traveling with us now, for this wasn't the main highway leading east.

His eyes were closed, but I knew he wasn't sleeping, so I nudged him with my foot. "How come you're still with us? I thought you wanted to go east so you could earn a million dollars."

His eyes snapped open. "I'm going east so I can get a job and finish school." He shut his eyes again. "Million dollars," he growled, shaking his head.

"You could have finished school in Rider's Dock," I argued for the pure pleasure of annoying him.

"My pa and I had a disagreement about something," he said.

"Betty-Dean?" I asked.

He looked at me.

"I know you hid her in the barn," I said. "She told me so. Does your dad know where she is?"

"No. But I got sick of arguing about it so I left."

"And now you're on your way to Chicago," I said. "So how come you're here if we're going to Soap Lake?"

He sighed. "I'm in no hurry. And Abel needs help with the truck. He can't keep it running by himself. Satisfied?"

"No," I said. "Are you going to help us get Rider?"

"Why not?" he said. "Now stop talking so much. I'm trying to sleep."

The sun sank and we drove on into the dark that was scented with sage.

It was past ten o'clock when we reached Soap Lake, and Grandpa stopped at a campground where a low fire burned within a circle of a dozen cars. We parked between another truck and a sedan with all its doors open and the seats pulled out. The seats had been put down in front of the car and several small children, tangled together, slept on them, watched over by an old lady sitting in a folding canvas chair.

"Good evening," she said as we got out to stretch our cramped legs.

"Evening," Annie said. She nodded toward the fire, where several people sat. "Traveling together, are you?"

"No. We only met up here tonight, but we're friends, though. Most pickers know each other. Where are you bound?"

"We came to see Billy Bong's revival," Annie said, "but I guess we missed him."

"You didn't miss much, I heard tell back at the gas station. The folks around here don't think much of him and neither do I, if the truth must be told."

Annie leaned against the car fender. "Then I'll tell the truth, too," she said. "I hate the man, but someone's traveling with him that we need to see. Have you heard where he might be staying?"

The old woman shook her head. "No, never thought to ask. But they'll know at the gas station, I'll bet. It's closed now, but you can ask there in the morning."

I gritted my teeth to keep from groaning. The morning was a million hours away.

"You folks sit over there by the fire," the old woman said. "They've got hot coffee and doughnuts, and they're real nice people."

As she spoke, someone by the fire began singing and the others joined in. It was the most peaceful sight I'd ever seen, with the flames dying down in the warm night, and the people smiling as they sang gentle songs that Jonah would have loved, "In the Gloaming," "Juanita," and "Abide with Me." I couldn't help but sing along, and I heard Hank's familiar, clear voice, too, although I couldn't see him very well in the dark.

We sat down with the singing strangers and stayed until the last burning log collapsed with a tiny shower of scarlet sparks. Then Annie and I made our beds in the back of the truck while Grandpa and Hank rolled up in their blankets on the ground beside us. Overhead, the sky was splashed with stars, and somewhere, under those stars, my little brother slept.

"Rachel," Annie whispered, "if you made up your mind to dream true, you could."

I was too afraid to dream true. I slept at last, having made up my mind instead to dream no dreams at all.

Twelve

By six in the morning we were up and devouring breakfast with the other travelers. A young, freckled woman had given us a dozen fat ripe peaches, and the old lady next to us produced a sack of brown buns. We shared Mama's jam and apple butter with them until the jars were empty. Several families made coffee on camp stoves. Small children ran shouting and laughing everywhere, too young to know they were poor and vulnerable.

I brooded over my coffee. If I had known the name of Rider's father, I could have asked about him. Someone at the rest stop might know him. Most of them knew or had heard of Casey and were not the least bit surprised when Grandpa told how he'd helped us. Casey was everyone's hero.

No one had anything good to say about Billy Bong, though. He didn't have the reputation of giving, only taking, and he didn't hesitate to take from those who had almost nothing.

The gas station opened at seven and we were there, waiting.

"Fill her up," Grandpa told the attendant, and he aimed a kick at the truck. "And check her dingdonged oil, too. She's laying down a black cloud."

Hank dragged the water hose over and uncapped the radiator. "If you're going to wash up in the john, you'd better hurry," he grumbled. "We can't wait all day while you primp."

I had no intention of leaving the scene until I heard Grandpa ask about Billy Bong, so I raised my chin and said, "I'm clean enough. But you look like you've been digging potatoes."

Hank flushed, but I didn't care. However, I moved away before he could comment on my rumpled clothes.

"Is Billy Bong's revival still in town?" Grandpa asked the attendant, pretending a great interest in one of the many dents in the truck's fenders.

The attendant spat on the ground. "They left last night, and good riddance to them."

"Oh, no," I whispered. Suddenly Rider seemed as far away as the moon.

"But they had that big tent," Annie cried. "You mean they packed it up in the dark and left?"

"It was an open-air service. Real short. They didn't have more than fifty people show up," he said with satisfaction. "And half of them were the sheriff and his men and some of the others around here who have their own reasons for wanting that bunch of thieves out of town as fast as possible."

"You were there?" Grandpa asked.

"No. But the sheriff's my cousin and he told me about it."

"Did he happen to mention if Pearl Sweet was with Billy Bong?" Grandpa asked.

The attendant wiped his hands on a stained rag. "His sister? Where you find Billy, you'll find her. She a friend of yours?"

"Someone we know is traveling with her," Annie told the man. "We'd like to catch up with them if we can."

"Easy," the man said. "They'll be in Ritzville tomorrow."

"So we heard," Grandpa said. "But where will they be staying tonight?"

The man shrugged. "Could be anywhere between here and Ritzville. Odessa, maybe. Or maybe they have friends at one of the big ranches. Keep an eye out for that white bus."

Grandpa nodded. "We'll do that. Now what do I owe you?"

The man calculated carefully, writing on the post next to him with the stub of a pencil. "Gas and oil, a dollar thirty." He looked around at all four of us and added, "If you're interested, I can let you have a sack of apples and we'll call it an even buck fifty. My wife's father raises the best apples around."

"We can use them," Annie murmured quickly. "There's not an awful lot of food left, Abel."

"The sack of apples and a bottle of new cider," the man said when Grandpa hesitated. "The cider's not hard," he added, seeing Annie's scowl.

"Done," Grandpa said, and he produced a dollar bill and a fifty-cent piece.

Once we were on our way again, I gave in to my despair. Rider was slipping farther away from us. Panic sparked in

127

me and I could not make myself comfortable, no matter how much I shifted around. "Watch for the white bus," I said to Hank.

"I'll watch," he said. "I wish you'd quit thinking about the ways we can fail instead of all the ways we can get Rider back."

"How do you know what I'm thinking?" I demanded.

He looked at me soberly. "I always know."

"Do not," I argued.

He sighed and looked away. He was tanned as brown as Grandpa, and his dark hair needed cutting. His hands were strong and lean, with long fingers. He must have felt me studying him, because his gaze met mine suddenly and we both flushed.

"You do not know what I'm thinking," I cried.

"Don't you wish I didn't," he scoffed, and then he enraged me by laughing.

I scrambled toward him, my hand raised to slap him silly, but he grabbed my arm and held it.

"You're wearing a skirt, Rachel," he growled, "so act like a girl for once."

Grandpa tooted the horn, and when I turned my head, I saw him glaring back at us over his shoulder. "Damned kids!" he bellowed. "Quit that fighting or I'll knock your heads together."

Hank let go of my arm, and I sank back in my place.

"I hate and despise and loathe you, Hank Webster," I hissed.

"I know," he said. His mouth wasn't smiling but his eyes were, and suddenly I wanted to throw myself at him, wind my arms around his neck, and kiss him better than Maysie had.

"You don't know anything!" I shouted.

He shrugged, grinning, then looked away and didn't look back.

A scorching wind tore at the stiff sage that grew beside the road, and where there were cultivated fields, the wheat rippled like golden water. We saw few farmhouses and no white bus anywhere. Occasionally a car would pass and leave us laboring behind. The truck engine clattered and groaned, and I wished a thousand times that Grandpa had been willing to borrow Cousin Jacob's truck.

"The engine sounds awful," I said. "What's wrong with it?"

"Everything," Hank said.

"Are we going to make it to Ritzville?"

Hank hesitated a second too long before he said, "Sure, so quit nattering at me."

I needed reassurance of some sort. "Will the truck hold up long enough for us to get Rider?"

"Yes!" he shouted at me. "We're going to get him!"

I stared and he subsided. "But I don't know if the truck can last long enough to get us home," he added wearily.

Fear flickered in me like summer lightning. I swallowed hard. "We'll manage something, once we get Rider away from them."

Hank, watching me, shook his head. "That could be the worst part. What if they come after us?"

My stomach hurt. I'd wondered that myself. "We can't let them see us, that's all," I said. "If we're careful, they won't know until it's too late. We'll do to them what they did to us."

"Set a fire? Are you crazy?"

"No!" I cried. "I mean we'll sneak Rider away — if we can. And if something goes wrong and we can't, then I'm just going to grab him and run. Maybe they won't go after us. They aren't so stupid that they'd go to the police, not after Rider was reported missing all over the state. That would be the same thing as confessing that they stole him to begin with."

"Who knows whose side the police would take?" Hank grumbled. "Anyway, Billy's got other ways of doing things."

"The men in the black suits," I said.

"They stole Rider in the first place. I don't think they'd mind doing it again. Are you ready for that?"

I took a deep breath. "Grandpa should have brought his gun."

Hank laughed bitterly. "That gun's broken. Abel doesn't even have any shells for it."

"Maybe we should have borrowed Betty-Dean's gun."

Hank's gaze was fixed on something far away. "Maybe. She's not going to have much use for it."

"I know. She told me she has cancer. Isn't there anything anybody can do?"

"No. That's why I brought her to the farm. She wants to die in a quiet place without anybody yelling at her. An animal deserves that much."

"But she's not going to die that soon!" I protested. "She's going to leave the farm in a few days, as soon as her ankle heals."

"She won't be leaving," Hank said abruptly.

It took a moment before I understood him. "You mean she's going to die right away? At the farm? Does Grandpa know that?"

"Grandpa and your cousins."

"But what's Mama going to do? If they call the funeral parlor . . . " I couldn't go on. The mere thought of Mama having to deal with the body of a murderer scared me speechless. If she was too fragile to be told that Betty-Dean was there in the first place, how could Grandpa have left the farm knowing that Mama might have to deal with a body?

"Your mama won't know," Hank said. "It's all worked out. And I don't want to talk about it anymore."

"You have to talk about it!" I cried. "What do you mean, Mama won't know? As soon as the undertaker comes for the body, the police will find out and they'll tell Mama."

"Nobody's going to call the undertaker. Jacob and I dug a grave where Abel showed us. The cousins can take care of everything else."

"Betty-Dean's going to be buried on the farm?" I exclaimed. "Are you crazy? They can't do that."

"Can and will," Hank said. "Now I told you more than I should have, so remember you're Abel Chance's granddaughter and keep the secret. Forever."

"But Hank . . . " I began.

He reached out one hand and took mine. "Betty-Dean's problems are almost over. You've got your own problems. Big ones."

He let go of my hand, and I looked away. If I let myself think about it too much, everything seemed hopeless and stealing Rider back seemed beyond anything we could accomplish.

"I'm getting hungry," I said, to change the subject, and I knocked on the truck roof over Grandpa's head. When he glanced back, I shouted, "Let's stop somewhere and eat!"

He nodded, and soon after that, we pulled up to a gas station connected to a small store. Grandpa's limp was worse now, but when Annie asked him about it, he scowled and stumped over to watch the attendant top off the gas tank.

While Hank examined the truck's newest tire, Annie and I bought loaves of fresh bread and half of a summer sausage in the store. Annie and the woman who waited on us were comparing recipes for herbal tea and "drawing" poultices, so I let down the truck's tailgate and used it as a table while I made sandwiches.

The woman from the store followed Annie out to the porch. "I've got cold lemonade made up, if that sounds good to you folks."

My mouth watered, but I wasn't certain if we could afford anything else. The woman saw our discomfort, so she said, "It's to pay Annie for the advice she gave me."

I drank lemonade until I felt as if I sloshed when I walked. When we moved on, nothing seemed impossible to me. The people we'd met up with so far had been wonderful to us, generous and helpful even though times were hard for them, too. When I saw that Hank had fallen asleep across from me, I didn't even kick him to wake him up. For a little while, the world seemed like a good place.

And then we came on the scene of the accident.

One car lay on its side next to the road. The other car had skidded past it, scattering broken glass. One of the doors was open, and a woman lay half out of it.

Grandpa stopped and Hank and I leaped out and ran. Hank knelt beside the woman first, then he yelled, "Rachel, stay back."

But I didn't. The woman was dead, her face crushed. I turned away.

Grandpa limped up. "Dead?"

Hank nodded. "But there's a guy in the car. Let's look."

Annie was peering in the window of the other car. "There's a man in here," she cried. "And a little girl."

I ran back to help, but they weren't moving. The windshield looked as if both of them had been flung headfirst into it.

Annie was struggling to open the driver's door, but it was jammed shut. I opened the other door and leaned inside. When I touched her, the little girl groaned.

"She's alive!" I yelled.

Annie and I lifted her carefully and put her down in the grass beside the road. Then I crawled back in the car to look closely at the man. He was breathing, but he was too large for us to move.

While Annie tended to the child, I ran back to the other car. Grandpa and Hank had pulled a man out, but Grandpa waved me back. "There's nothing to be done."

Another car stopped beside us, and the driver said he'd find a telephone and call for help. As he disappeared down the hot, shimmering road, I asked Grandpa how far away the help was.

Grandpa, spreading his handkerchief over the dead man's face, said, "Far enough so that you'd better start praying."

The hot wind blew, and the terrible scorched sky smothered us. The unconscious little girl groaned sometimes, and once she cried "Daddy!" Tears filled my eyes and I stumbled away. Alone, a hundred yards down the empty road, I knelt and wept until I was exhausted. Why didn't someone come? How could such a hideous thing happen?

At last I heard a siren in the distance, and I got to my feet. Behind me, Hank rose up also.

"How long have you been there?" I asked, humiliated.

He blinked and I saw that his lashes were wet. "Long enough to make sure you didn't aggravate a rattlesnake." His voice was rough and thick, and I knew that he was as embarrassed to be caught crying as I was. "Come on, Rachel. Let's see if we can give them a hand."

The men from the ambulance knew the man and little girl. "It's Collie Henderson and her pa," one of them told us. "They're my neighbors in Odessa."

I felt better that the child was being taken away by a friend. The ambulance roared off, siren screaming, and passed a sheriff's car coming toward us.

The officers covered the bodies with blankets, asked us many questions, and finally thanked us for stopping and helping. They knew little Collie Henderson and her father, too, and seemed truly worried about them. I couldn't help but think how different they were from Chief Carmichael, who didn't worry about anyone.

We left the officers there and turned toward Odessa again, reaching it an hour later. On the far side of the small

134

town, we stopped at a campground. Puzzled, Hank and I jumped down.

"Why are we stopping?" I asked Grandpa. "We could go miles before dark."

'Abel's leg is hurting," Annie said. "We'll stop for the night here."

"My leg is fine!" Grandpa shouted. "If you'd give me back my bottle, maybe it'd be even finer."

Annie didn't bother to reply. She opened the passenger door and struggled out of the seat. "Hank, you clear out the back of the truck so we can make a bed for Abel and prop up his bad leg. Rachel, open up my suitcase. I'm going to show you how to make a poultice."

"I'm not going to bed," Grandpa said, grim and scowling. "I'm going to heat me up the last two cans of beans and eat 'em all myself, since none of you seem to be hungry. And then, like it or not, we're going on to Ritzville."

"Tomorrow morning we're going to Ritzville," Annie barked. "Don't you argue with me, old man. If you behave, maybe I'll give you a sip from that bottle of poison. If you don't, I'll smash it on the ground right now."

Hank had already begun pulling our belongings out of the truck. I took the suitcase and opened it in the shade of the truck. Don't worry, I told myself. There will be plenty of time. Grandpa will feel better with a good rest. Rider, you mustn't be scared. We're coming closer all the time.

But the hot and dusty afternoon offered no promise of anything more encouraging than an endless continuation of our misery. The little camp stove seemed to fry my skin as I hovered over it, watching the poultice stew in the pan. Grandpa cursed under his breath as Hank helped him into the back of the truck, and Hank, grumpy himself, snarled back at Grandpa. When the day cooled, we ate bread and beans, and Grandpa finally fell asleep.

Other people came at twilight, but they weren't as friendly as the ones we'd stayed with the night before. There was no fire or singing, and our sleep was disturbed by wailing babies and men who argued bitterly over whether the United States should enter the war that was half a world away from us.

Annie slept next to me on the hard ground, and once she awoke with a cry.

"What's wrong?" I whispered. "Did you have a bad dream?"

"I dreamed of Pearl Sweet," she whispered. "She'd changed Rider's name. She was calling him by the name of her dead baby. And he wouldn't come to me when I called him Rider."

"She had a baby who died?" I raised up on my elbow. "Is that true?"

"Not that I know of," Annie said, sighing. "It was only a nightmare. I couldn't have been dreaming true. I'm too tired. Go back to sleep, Rachel."

But I lay awake considering something new. Of course Pearl Sweet would change Rider's name. He was so young, only two. And he'd been gone for so long that maybe he might have forgotten his real name if he never heard it anymore.

And perhaps he was forgetting us.

✼Thirteen

In the morning, we ate by ourselves. No one at the campground seemed to be sharing anything with anyone, not even conversation.

Grandpa's leg had swollen during the night. His face was gray under his tan, and through gritted teeth he urged us to hurry.

"Let me drive today," Hank said in a matter-of-fact voice.

I hoped Grandpa would forget his pride and give in. But he didn't.

"I'll drive," he said abruptly, jerking open the truck door. Annie gave me a look that expressed both exasperation and concern.

"Hank's getting tired of sitting in the back, Grandpa," I said, trying a different approach.

"Then let him lie down," Grandpa said, slamming his door shut.

We ran out of gas less than a mile later. Hank checked the tank with a long stick to make sure, and Grandpa exploded.

"Somebody siphoned the tank while we slept!" he

shouted, his face purple. "If I catch him, I'll drag him be-hind the dingbusted truck for ten miles!"

Annie coaxed him to lie on a blanket in the shade of the truck by offering him a gulp of his whiskey. I knew how much she hated to do that, but Grandpa quieted down and agreed to let her make him another poultice for his leg while Hank and I found a gas station.

As soon as we got out of earshot, Hank said, "When they can't see us anymore, I'll give you a lesson in hitchhiking."

"You know how Grandpa feels about riding with strangers."

"It'll save time," Hank said, looking back. "As soon as we get around this next curve, we'll give it a try."

"Only two cars have passed since we started out," I grumbled.

"And we're going to let a lot more pass. We're watching for a truck. We'll ride in back — it's safer. If the driver pulls off the main road, we can jump out."

I stared at him. "How come you know so much about this?"

"I hitch back and forth to Seattle all the time."

"What for?"

"Looking for work."

"You've been planning to quit school?" I exclaimed. "What kind of job could you find in Seattle?"

Hank sighed. "Night work, maybe, cleaning stores or offices. That way I could go to school, too. But nothing turned up and I had to get away from Pa."

"Because he got mad when you defended Betty-Dean," I volunteered. Then I remembered Mr. Webster's face the night he came looking for Hank. "Did the two of you get into a fight?"

Hank shrugged.

"Did he hurt you? Is that why you left?"

"You talk too much!" Hank cried, suddenly furious. "Look, here comes a flatbed truck. That'll be perfect."

We stuck out our thumbs and the ancient truck rattled to a halt. Hank told the driver where we were going, then leaped in back and pulled me up beside him. We sat together with our legs dangling, and the truck rumbled onward.

"See?" he said. "That's all there is to it. But never stand too close when the driver stops. Keep out of reach. If somebody tries something, like grabbing you, run back the way you came. They can't go after you unless they make a U-turn."

"Did anybody ever try anything with you?" I asked, fascinated.

"No," he said, "but it's a long way to Chicago."

"Why are you going there?"

"I heard that factory jobs are opening up."

"But I thought you wanted to go to school."

He glanced at me, then looked away. "I'll finish school. Right now it's first things first. After we get Rider, I'll take off and find a job, and then I'll think about school."

"You've got almost everything planned out," I said enviously. "I can't think past today."

"That's because Rider's your brother," Hank said. "You're too close to see the whole rotten world at one time."

I slumped. "Thanks," I said. "You're lots of fun."

"Quit worrying. If Rider's with Billy Bong, we'll get him back. Don't think about losing. Think about how strong and tough you are. Everything will work out."

"Do you really believe that?"

But Hank didn't answer. The truck stopped at a gas station and the driver tooted his horn. We jumped down and the truck labored away.

We weren't so lucky going back with the can of gas. We didn't see a truck, only cars. Half a dozen passed us, and one driver even stopped to ask if we wanted a ride, but Hank told the fat, pink man that we needed exercise. The man hesitated, looking at me, and I bent swiftly and picked up a rock. He drove on, scowling.

"You weren't going to throw that rock," Hank said, laughing.

"I had a clear shot at him through the open car window," I said, tossing the rock from one hand to the other. "You know I could have bounced this off his skull, no problem."

"It's better to turn and run," Hank said seriously.

But I kept the rock, just in case.

When Grandpa saw us coming, he peeled the poultice off his shin and pulled down his trouser leg. "It's about time," he said. "That poison Annie cooked up for my leg hurts worse than that old busted bone ever did. Gas up the truck, Hank, and let's get out of here before she tries to feed us poultice for lunch."

To my astonishment, he tossed the truck key to Hank. Hank caught it and pocketed it without comment. I looked to Annie for an explanation of this surrender, and she made a motion, behind Grandpa's back, of tilting a bottle to her lips several times. I understood. Grandpa was well on his way to being drunk, and he never drove then.

It was past lunchtime when we reached Ritzville, but we didn't stop to eat. There were signs and banners everywhere announcing the revival — and the time set for it wasn't six o'clock, as we'd thought. The service had begun at ten that morning.

"He can't be finished already," I said. "It's only been going on for a couple of hours."

"Knock on the cab and tell Hank to hurry," Grandpa said, ignoring me. "Billy could be packing up to leave."

This revival wasn't being preached inside a tent. When we arrived, we saw that a stage had been set up in a field. A choir sang a benediction as people streamed away. In a few minutes the field would be empty of everything but the stage and the yelling choir. Billy Bong and his attendants were nowhere in sight.

"It's over," I said, despairing.

Hank stopped the truck and I jumped out to talk to him. "Billy Bong won't be out of town yet," I said. "The people are just leaving, so he's around somewhere. Look for the white bus."

I climbed in with Grandpa, and Hank eased the truck back into the traffic surging both ways on the narrow street. After three or four blocks, I caught a glimpse of the bus down a side street, and I hammered on the cab roof and yelled at Hank to turn right. We circled back around the block, and sure enough, there was Billy Bong's bus, parked in front of what looked like a big boarding house.

Hank slowed down and we took a good, long look. The

front door of the house was open, but I couldn't see anyone inside. Hank parked the truck around the corner and I got out.

"Rider must be there," I said to Hank. I was shaking.

"We don't know that," Hank said. "Pearl may be staying somewhere else. But let's go take a look."

Grandpa wanted to get out, too, but I told him the simple, cruel truth. "Hank and I can go faster. We'll come back and tell you what we see before we do anything."

We walked close together in silence. As we turned the corner, a car pulled up in front of the house. A man in a black suit got out and hurried up the steps. Billy Bong stepped out on the porch and spoke to the man. He was in his shirtsleeves, holding a bottle of Coca-Cola in one hand. The man nodded, said a few words, and then ran back down the steps.

"Pearl Sweet's in that car," Hank whispered.

I saw her in the passenger seat and I started forward, but Hank grabbed my arm. "No," he said. "Watch."

The man started the car and drove toward the corner. I saw Pearl Sweet's flat, perspiring face, her faint smile.

And in the moment it took for the car to pass us, I saw a small, dark-haired boy in her lap.

"It wasn't Rider," Hank said.

"It was!" I exclaimed. I dug my fingers into Hank's arm. "Quick! Let's follow them! It was Rider!"

"Rider's blond," Hank said, staring at me as if I'd lost my mind. "That little kid had dark hair, like mine."

"They've dyed it," I said, dragging him into a half run. "I don't care what they've done to him, I know my brother."

I scrambled back in the truck and told Grandpa what we'd seen.

"Are you sure?" he asked me.

"I'm absolutely certain." I banged on the truck roof and Hank started the engine.

As soon as we turned off that quiet street, we were caught in the traffic leaving the revival site. The car with Rider was out of sight. I stood in the back of the truck, leaning on the cab, looking everywhere. Dust burned my eyes. The hideous noon sun turned the sky white. The metal beneath my fingers scorched them until I had to let go.

I sat back down with Grandpa. "What did you see?" he asked.

"We lost them."

"Then we'll find them again. At least now we know for certain that Pearl Sweet's got Rider." He mopped his forehead with his handkerchief. "You are sure, aren't you?"

"I'm sure," I said. "Why didn't I just climb in that car and grab him? Why did I stand there gawking?"

Grandpa grasped my hand. "That wouldn't have worked. Sometime today they'll leave for Pasco because the list Millie gave you says they've got a church breakfast there tomorrow. We'll be there, too."

There was no point in sitting there watching the bus. We were hungry and hot, so we found a roadside fruit and vegetable stand outside of town and spent a dollar on fresh peaches, watermelon, corn, and potatoes. A mile or so farther on, we stopped for a meal.

Grandpa, who'd been sleeping, woke with a cry when Annie slammed the passenger door.

"It's all right, Abel," she said. "We're stopping for lunch."

We weren't at a campground, only a wide parking place beside the road, and another car was already there. Farther down the road, I saw a sprawling farm workers' camp, with row after row of shacks so dismal that we wouldn't have allowed our chickens to enter them.

"I'd rather sleep right here than in one of those places," I told Annie.

"They're terrible, all right," she said as she opened her suitcase and took out the stove. "But the people are safer there than they might be some places. Like here, for instance. And if we slept here and the police came along, we'd be in trouble anyway. Seems that it's a crime to be too poor to spend the night in a motor court."

"I hate all this!" I blurted. I slammed a saucepan on the ground. "I never knew we were *poor* before. I thought only that we didn't have much money."

My outburst startled everyone. "There are worse things than being poor," Grandpa said quietly.

"Like what?" I shouted. "If we'd been rich, don't you know that everybody would have cared when Rider was stolen? The police would have swarmed over the whole state looking for him!"

"Being rich didn't help the Lindberghs," Annie said. "Their little boy died."

That shut me up. Ashamed, I bent to pick up the sauce-pan.

We made plans while we ate. "If we skip Pasco and go

straight to Yakima, we can be there before Billy Bong," Grandpa said.

Hank nodded. "There'd be plenty of time, even if we have more trouble with the truck."

"Hush," Annie said. "Don't say it out loud."

Grandpa scowled at her. "You think the truck's listening?" He rubbed his leg for a moment, and then began laughing. "Maybe you're right. It's sitting over there eavesdropping and planning what it's going to do to us next."

"Ha," Hank said gloomily. "I can believe it."

While Hank helped Grandpa get settled in the back of the truck again, Annie and I crossed the highway to a gas station to use the women's rest room. I felt unbearably grubby, but I did the best I could to get clean at the washbasin. My new skirt and blouse were soiled in spite of my efforts to keep them clean, and I wished that I'd taken Mama's advice and brought an extra pair of overalls.

When we were done, Annie said she wanted to give the man at the gas station a nickel for letting us use the rest room, so I waited next to the gas pump while she trotted inside the station. A new pickup truck pulled up and two young men got out.

"Well, well, what have we here?" one of them said. He circled around me, grinning. "All by yourself, sweetie?"

I looked up into his pale, oily face. "Go away," I said.

He laughed, and the other fellow reached out to touch my hair. I jerked away.

"She's skittish as a cat," the pale one said.

"She needs some fun. We know what to do about that,

don't we?" his friend said. He winked at me. "How about going for a ride in my new truck? Would you like that?"

I glanced quickly into the station. Annie was talking to the man inside. I started toward the door, but the pale man grabbed my arm and held it tightly.

"Let go," I growled.

He laughed, and almost simultaneously, I jammed my free hand into his face, digging in my fingernails. He yelped and let go of me, to clap both his hands over his face.

"She clawed me!" He pulled his hands away and looked at them. "I'm bleeding." He lunged at me then, and grabbed me before I could get inside the door.

I had only one arm free, but I used it, pounding his head with my fist, but he was too strong and he dragged me toward the truck. The other fellow held the passenger door open. Neither of them was laughing any longer. Behind me I heard Annie scream.

I'd been shoved halfway into the truck when the pale man dropped to the ground like a stone. Hank stood over him, holding a rock the size of a brick in one hand.

"You've killed him!" the other man yelled.

"Not yet, but that comes next," Hank said. He pulled me away from the truck. "Get that pig out of here before I finish the job," he said to the man.

The gas station operator had come out with Annie, and he was holding a rifle. "I'll tell you once more, Clarence," he said to the owner of the truck, "stay away from here or I'll do to you what your dad should have done a long time ago."

"I won't forget this, Eddie," Clarence said as he shoved his groaning friend into the truck.

"You'd forget your name if your mama didn't embroider it on your bloomers," Eddie said. He raised the rifle. "Clear out."

Clarence slammed the passenger door and looked straight at Hank. "We'll be back for you."

"If your mother lets you," Hank said quietly.

The truck roared away, and I relaxed, shaking Hank's hand loose from mine.

"Is that your truck across the road?" Eddie asked.

We nodded.

"I'd move on if I was you," Eddie said. "Those boys are trouble."

Everything is trouble, I thought as I made myself comfortable next to Grandpa in the back of the truck. People, weather, machinery. I was sore and tired, and sick of being scared.

Tomorrow, I said to Rider in my mind. Tomorrow is the day I find you. In my imagination, I saw him reach out his arms and I heard him say, "Sis, pick me up."

"Yes," I whispered. "Tomorrow."

✣ Fourteen

The truck broke down outside Othello. Grandpa and I had been sleeping, and the silence woke me. The grinding, laboring engine had stopped.

Hank, scowling and muttering, was clearly in no mood to answer my questions. Annie sat on the running board, fanning herself with a road map, and when she saw that I was awake and on my feet, she said, "Don't fret, Rachel. Hank will get us going again right away."

Hank looked up from the engine. "No," he said. "You might as well look around for a good place to set up for the night, because I don't know how long this will take."

"But you will get it fixed, won't you?" I asked. "We're not stuck here?"

He wiped his forehead with the back of his hand. "We'll get Rider, no matter what. I'm not so sure that I can fix this truck."

"But we've got to . . . " I began.

Grandpa, hopping on his good leg and steadying himself with one hand on the truck, joined us. "Rachel, there's a gas station down the road. Looks like the owner might live in back. Go ask him if we can bed down on the other side of those trees behind the station. If we can't stay at a campground, we'll be better off on private property. That way we won't catch the attention of the wrong people."

I knew he was thinking about the men who'd tried to grab me. We were miles away, but maybe that wasn't far enough.

Annie decided to go with me. "Don't worry," she told me when we got far enough away so Grandpa and Hank couldn't hear us. "They'll think of something, and if they don't, we'll leave the truck here and find another way to get to Yakima."

I walked head down, watching my shoes kick up dust. "Sometimes I think we weren't meant to have Rider back. Everything's going wrong."

Annie grabbed my hand and squeezed it hard. "Stop that right now! I know you'll get Rider back. I saw it again an hour ago, and I was seeing true."

I didn't know whether or not to believe her. Druid Annie did see true sometimes. Everybody knew that. But she admitted that her fortunetelling was half fake. Was this one of the fake times?

The man at the gas station saw us coming and walked out to greet us. "I saw your trouble up the road there," he said. "Is there anything I can do?"

"Our menfolk say the truck won't get us any farther today," Annie said. "Would you let us spend the night on your property?" She cocked her head toward me. "We don't fancy sleeping beside the road. We could pay you a quarter, and another quarter if you let us use enough of your water to wash up good for once."

The man was as old as Grandpa, and even thinner. "You can camp back there free if you clean up after yourselves," he said. "Water's free, too. And I'll work on your truck, if the men want me to, but I'll have to charge for that." While he spoke, one hand restlessly moved over a terrible scar on his neck. He saw me looking and I felt myself blush with embarrassment.

"A souvenir from the big war," he said. "I'll go take a look at your truck."

We thanked him for his kindness and spent a few minutes in his immaculate rest room. There was even a shower in one corner, but the water was cold.

"Paradise," Annie said, sighing happily.

I nodded but I was thinking about the man's scar. War, poverty, lost children, abused wives. What a fearful and ugly world we lived in. And how sad it was that we thought that the promise of a cold shower was paradise.

When we came out, the man's wife was minding the station for him. He'd taken his truck up the highway to tow ours back.

"My name's Aurora Carpenter," she told us.

"I'm Druid Annie and this is Rachel," Annie said. "We're grateful to your husband for his kindness."

The woman looked down the road reflectively. "He'll do, better than most." She turned to study Annie. "What did you say your name was?"

"Annie."

"You said something else first."

"She's called Druid Annie," I offered.

The woman nodded. "My mother was called Druid

Bess," she said. "She was Welsh and she knew everything there was to know about healing."

"So does Annie," I said.

The two women looked into each other's eyes. "I'll have a word with you, then," Aurora said. "There's a lady nearby that I can't help. But I don't know everything my mama knew."

They went inside the station and sat on stools, talking eagerly. I watched the trucks in the distance, the occasional car that passed, and the dust devils dancing beside the road.

Don't be scared, Rider, I thought. But I was sick with fear.

The Carpenters shared their dinner with us, and we all ate at a rough table under the trees while the blazing sun sank. The men discussed the truck in low voices, scowling as they scraped the last bits of stew from their plates. I listened, depressed, while Shorty Carpenter explained that he'd need to go back to Ritzville in the morning for the part they needed. He wouldn't estimate how long it would take to repair the truck.

"I'll try to have you on your way by tomorrow night," he said.

Tomorrow night. No, I thought. That's too late. Tomorrow has to be the day we find Rider. We can't go on like this much longer.

The men worked on the truck until the last of the light was gone, and then the Carpenters went inside. We took turns showering in the cold water, then Annie and I made up beds for all of us under the trees. Over our heads, the sky was a glittering mass of stars. The night was silent except for an occasional passing car.

I lay between Grandpa and Annie, thinking, questioning myself, despairing, then planning. After a while I heard Grandpa snore. It took longer for Annie's breathing to even out and soften. Hank, on the far side of the truck, was probably already asleep.

At last I rose silently and picked up my shoes. Carefully, one step at a time, I made my way to the truck, where my jacket lay in the back. I pulled it on, checking my pockets for my birthday dollar and the precious piece of paper with Rider's handprint on it, my talisman against loneliness.

Watch for me tomorrow, Rider, I thought.

I took one step, and a hand closed around my ankle.

Hank! I aimed a kick at him, but he rolled to one side and leaped up, quiet as a cat.

"Where are you going?" he whispered.

"To the rest room," I lied.

"You're running off." He grabbed my arm and pulled me with him, toward the other side of the trees. "Are you crazy? Why are you doing this?"

I yanked free of him. "I'm going after Rider."

"We'll have the truck working again by noon."

"You will not," I said. "Shorty won't be back with the part by then."

"We'll get the truck fixed and be in Yakima in time for the revival."

I clenched my fists. "I won't take any more chances on that truck!"

"So you'll get there faster by walking?"

"I'll hitchhike."

"That's stupid! You're a girl. It's not safe. Yakima's seventy miles away, maybe more." He reached for me again but I dodged him.

"I'm going and you can't stop me. Nobody can stop me. If I can't get away from you tonight, I'll get away tomorrow. One way or another."

"Then I'm coming, too," Hank said.

"You can't! They need you to help fix the truck. And Grandpa can't drive anymore."

"Listen to me for a minute. What are you going to do, even if you make it to Yakima? Grab Rider by yourself? How will you get away with him? Have you thought about that?"

"I've thought of everything," I said, but that was a lie. I hadn't thought past grabbing Rider the next time I saw him and running for our lives.

"How will you get back home?" Hank asked, with horrible practicality.

"Hitchhike," I said.

"With a little kid?"

"We'll take a bus."

"Do you have enough money?"

We both knew that my birthday dollar wasn't taking Rider and me home. "Give me your money, then," I said.

Hank dug through his pocket and took out a dollar bill and a handful of change. "This won't be enough, either," he said.

Ah, I thought. He's talking now as if he accepts the fact that I'm leaving. All we have to do is make a better plan for Rider and me to get away.

"Okay," I said, "what shall I do instead?"

"Well, you can't wake up Abel and Annie and ask them for money," he said. "Look. Do it this way. If — no, when! — you get Rider, start walking toward Ellensburg, but keep off the main road until dark. Then walk on the left, facing traffic, because that's safer."

"Because anybody following us who tried to grab us would have to make a U-turn first," I said, showing him how much I knew about the rules of traveling by foot on long and lonely roads.

"Right. Keep your eyes open. We'll be on our way by dark for sure, and we'll keep driving until we find you. Just be sure you're on the main road by dark."

The highway between Yakima and Ellensburg stretched out forever in my imagination. Could I really do it?

"And if you don't get Rider — " Hank began.

That was all I needed. "I'll get him!"

We were silent for a moment, facing each other in the dark. "This is crazy," he said. "It won't work. You can't do it alone. You're a girl! Remember those guys who gave you the bad time? There are other guys just like them. And there are all of Billy Bong's people, too."

"It'll work because I am a girl all alone," I said, suddenly certain. "It'll work because nobody would believe I'd try it all by myself."

"Abel's going to kill me when he finds out I knew you were leaving," Hank said.

"Then don't tell him. Be surprised when he wakes up in the morning and finds out I'm gone." I was growing braver by the moment. "Hank, by tomorrow this time, it'll all be over. We'll be on our way back to Rider's Dock with my brother."

154

"Sure," Hank said. I couldn't tell if he really believed me. "Be careful and don't trust anybody. Remember what I taught you about hitchhiking. And keep a sharp rock in your hand. Nobody's got better aim than you."

He had finally admitted it. "Thanks," I said. I turned to go, then I stopped. "I'm counting on you to find us," I said.

"I'll find you, Rachel," he said. "No matter where you are."

Satisfied, I walked through the night with the stars blazing above me and a clean wind refreshing my soul. I felt fully alive and powerful, as if I were a part of everything. Throughout all of the universe, galaxies were swinging in their appointed courses. The seasons would continue to come and go. And it seemed to me in my innocence that, according to a plan set at the beginning of time, my brother and I would plant bluebells on Betty-Dean's grave next spring.

Dawn came early, and shortly afterward a cabbage truck stopped for me. I climbed up in back and sat on the cabbages, watching morning unfold around me, all peach and rose, as we rushed toward Yakima.

The driver and his wife treated me to coffee at a diner in town. "Why did you want to come to Yakima?" the woman asked me.

"I'm meeting my brother here," I said.

"Oh, that's good," she said. "I hate to think of a young girl being on her own. But your brother will take care of you."

"He sure will," I said. I thanked them for the ride and the coffee and went on my way.

Watch for me, Rider.

✤ Fifteen

The morning sun shone on the main streets where blue banners swayed. The words "Tabernacle of Holy Enlightenment" were printed in elaborate gold letters on the bright strips of cloth. I didn't see Billy Bong's name anywhere, but I knew he was there. And so was Rider. I felt his presence.

It was too early for most stores to open, but I saw a woman coming out of a coffee shop on the corner, and I hurried to catch up with her.

"Ma'am?" I said. "Please, can you tell me where I can find the revival?" I pointed at the nearest banner.

She stopped and looked at me levelly. "That tabernacle bunch?"

I nodded. "Billy Bong's people."

Her mouth drew down. "Do your folks know you're interested in them? I wouldn't let a daughter of mine go near them."

"I don't want anything to do with them," I blurted hastily when she made an abrupt move to walk on. "But someone I know is traveling with them and I want to talk to him."

"He'd be better off if you dragged him away and pounded some sense into him," she said. "There's a perfectly decent church right at the end of this street, if it's churching he wants."

"Yes, ma'am," I said. "But do you know where the tabernacle people are holding the services?"

She sighed. "Turn right at the corner and keep walking. It's a long way, but you can't miss it. Just follow those white arrows on the telephone poles."

"Thanks," I murmured sincerely.

"But the first service doesn't start until noon," she said. "I think there's another at six this evening."

"I heard that," I told her. Millie's list had included the times that Billy Bong would preach in Yakima. "You wouldn't know where the tabernacle people spent the night, would you?"

"No."

I thanked her again and she clopped off, her steps echoing in the quiet morning.

When I turned the corner, I saw the arrows. Almost every telephone pole had one, pointing ahead. "This way to salvation," they said in scarlet letters.

Stores began opening as I passed. More people walked along the sidewalks, and some smiled at me. I smiled back and marched on toward my salvation.

After a few blocks, I saw a familiar old bus pulling away from a gas station. Casey Shay! I hurried, hoping to see him and shout hello before he drove across the intersection.

My attention was fixed on the front of the bus as I caught up even with the last window in the back.

"Rachel! What are you doing here?" a man shouted.

I looked up at the window and felt as if all my breath had been knocked out. Rider's father was on Casey Shay's bus!

I let out a shriek and began running, but the bus pulled noisily away from me, coughing and backfiring. Rider's father leaned out of the window, still shouting, but I couldn't hear what he said.

There was no time for me to tell him about Rider, no time to tell him anything that complicated, because I couldn't run fast enough to overtake the bus. He was slipping out of my life again.

"Mama needs you!" I screamed. *"Mama needs you!"*

The bus turned the corner at the end of the block and roared away. Dust rolled back toward me. I slowed and stopped. Had he heard me?

No, probably not. I began crying so suddenly that I shocked myself. All the certainty I'd felt since I'd left Hank the night before shattered into bits.

Rider's father had been here and I had missed him! If I had only walked a little faster, I'd have found the bus still at the gas station. I could have told him everything, even if it meant breaking my word to Mama. He would have helped me get Rider back. He could have marched in and taken Rider any time, because Rider was his own boy! The nightmare would have been over, if only I had walked a little faster.

God was punishing me. Suddenly I understood exactly what Mama felt. Somehow I'd done something so bad that

Rider was always just out of reach. Over and over again, I'd missed him, and now the best chance I'd ever had to get him back had disappeared around the corner in Casey Shay's old bus.

Had God let all this happen because Rider was illegitimate and because I didn't care but loved him anyway? Or was it because I despised Pastor Woodie and wouldn't go to his church — or any other church? Or because I didn't tell the police that Betty-Dean was hiding, and dying, in our barn? Or because I'd wanted to kiss Hank?

Maybe I could strike a bargain with God. Could I stop loving Rider and start being ashamed of him? No. If I promised that, I'd be lying.

I could apologize to Pastor Woodie and go to his church. But the truth was that I'd still despise him.

There was no way I could turn in Betty-Dean. Never.

I hardly knew how I felt about Hank. If I concentrated, it might be possible to hate him as much as I'd always said I did. But somehow I was certain that God wouldn't be impressed with that.

Listen, I said to God in my mind, I don't know why any of this happened. All I know is that I've got to take my brother home. If You won't help me, or if You can't help me, then maybe You could try to forgive me for whatever I did and give me a little push in the right direction. I'll do my best to manage on my own after that and not pester You anymore. Amen.

I walked on, desolate. Weren't people supposed to feel good when they prayed? I hadn't had much experience, but I certainly didn't feel any better.

One more thing, God, I thought, certain that I was pestering Him now. If I fail, then could You maybe watch over my brother and let him be happy? You care about sparrows, so You must care about little boys. Amen for the second time.

Now I felt satisfied.

I found the revival site not long after that. The tent was up, and I heard the sounds of a practicing choir coming from inside. Several cars were parked nearby, but I didn't see the white bus. Or the car I'd seen carrying Pearl Sweet.

I walked past and circled a block, heading back toward the town's business district, looking for a place to eat. When I found a small diner, I bought a cheese sandwich and a glass of orange pop for twenty cents. That was too much money for such a small amount of food, but I paid without arguing. The people here probably raised their prices just as the people in Rider's Dock did when Billy Bong was in town.

After I ate, I hurried back to the revival. There were more parked cars now, and people were streaming into the tent. I didn't hear the choir, but someone was playing hymns on a piano.

A family with several children parked half a block away and strolled past me. I set out behind them, close enough to be mistaken for one of them, I hoped. No one paid attention to me when I followed them inside the tent.

They went straight to empty chairs halfway up the aisle. I sat in back, close to the entrance, just in case I needed to leave in a hurry.

There was a stage opposite the entrance, with a pulpit and a piano. And the screen that had hidden Billy Bong in Rider's Dock. A choir sat in back, next to the screen.

160

Then people began crowding in, and the tent was packed full within a very few minutes. A child somewhere cried and fussed.

Where was Pearl Sweet? I got to my feet so that I could see better. Had I missed her when she came in?

Half a dozen men in black suits filed in then and took their places in chairs at the foot of the platform. I watched them for a moment, and then looked back toward the entrance.

Pearl Sweet walked down the aisle, dressed in white, leading my brother by the hand. Rider, his hair dyed brown, wore white, too. He passed me so closely that I could have reached out and touched his sober little face.

My pulse hammered in my throat. For an instant, I considered grabbing him and running out of the tent. But this was too public a place. I'd be chased down and Rider would be taken away from me before I could explain.

I sat, willing myself to be calm. The woman next to me smiled and said, "It's exciting, isn't it?"

"Yes," I said.

"Have you been saved?" she asked.

"From what?" I blurted, thinking that she meant to ask if I'd been saved from capture by Billy Bong's people or the police.

She stared at me, then turned her face away. The services began with an embarrassing, out-of-tune shriek from the choir. I settled back in my chair to wait.

A local minister talked and talked. The air grew hot and thick. Women fanned themselves and men unbuttoned their suit jackets, while small children whined and wept.

At last Billy Bong stepped out from behind his screen, and I slid down in my chair, panicky and half-sick.

I knew there was no possibility that he could recognize me, but still I was afraid. Rider was out of sight, and all I could see of Pearl Sweet was the top of her head. For a few moments, I wondered if I'd lost my mind, coming here and expecting that I could take Rider back.

"Amen!" cried the woman next to me, in response to something Billy Bong was saying. "Amen!" yelled half of the audience.

Billy Bong introduced Pearl, then, and she got up to sing. She carried Rider and sat him down on the edge of the stage.

"Isn't he adorable?" the woman next to me said.

My fists clenched. "I didn't know she had children."

"Neither did I," she said. "But she could have adopted a child since the last time they were here."

Or stolen one, I thought.

The woman in front of us turned around and spoke to my neighbor. "That's her cousin's boy," she said. "The little fellow's mother is sick, so the Sweets have been taking care of him for the last few days. My sister knows Billy Bong's secretary, and that's what she told us."

I was listening so hard I forgot to breathe. Where had Rider been until a few days ago?

The woman next to me fanned herself with her large, flat purse. "Well, Pearl Sweet is a saint," she said. "She's been sick herself most of the summer, I heard. Billy had another singer with him in California."

I leaned close to her. "Where was Pearl staying when she was sick?" I asked, trying not to sound too eager.

The woman shrugged. "I don't believe I ever heard."

"Arizona," the woman in front of us said.

"Why would she go there?" my neighbor exclaimed, clearly prepared to argue.

"Shut up," the man next to her said. She scowled but obeyed.

Pearl finished her song, picked up Rider, and sat down in front of the platform again. Billy Bong came forward and began talking about the war orphans in London.

"They need clothes and food," he said. "Give us your money, every penny you can spare and then at least one dollar more, and we'll see that the little orphans have everything they need."

While the choir hummed, men in black suits passed collection plates down the long rows of chairs. I watched the plate in the row ahead of me, knowing that in a moment it would be handed back to my row. Grandpa said that Billy Bong kept all the money people gave him. I wasn't about to contribute a cent. If Hank couldn't fix the truck, or if he missed me on the road to Ellensburg, I'd have to find another way home.

But as the plate drew nearer to me, and I saw the heap of paper money in it, I decided that I needed bus fare much more than Billy Bong needed another silk shirt. I pulled out one of the two dollar bills in my pocket.

The plate was coming down my row. I held the dollar bill between my first two fingers and cupped my hand. With my left hand, I took the plate from my neighbor.

A folded bill lay on top. I lowered my hand over it, dropped my dollar bill, and palmed the folded one. Then I smiled up at the usher who was waiting for the plate. But he was looking ahead and I had to wait a moment before he took the plate. My smile was so stiff that my lips felt cracked.

After he walked away, I stole a glance into my closed fist. Five dollars. That would be more than enough for the bus, I thought. I leaned back in my chair and sighed deeply, then sat up again, alert as a cat.

Pearl Sweet was threading her way down the aisle between the ushers who were carrying their spoils toward the stage and the waiting Billy Bong. Rider, flushed and perspiring, rode solemnly in Pearl's arms, looking back over her shoulder. It took all of my willpower to keep from crying his name as he passed.

Pearl left the tent. I got to my feet and followed her outside. She strode purposefully across the street and put Rider down. Then, holding his hand, she slowed her pace and they walked away under the spreading branches of old shade trees. Neither of them saw me following half a block behind.

They turned left at the next corner. I began to run, then stopped. No matter how afraid I was that they'd disappear into a house without my knowing which one, I was even more afraid of Pearl seeing me too soon.

After an eternity passed, I turned the corner, too. Pearl and Rider were climbing the two steps to a broad porch. The house was the largest on the block, painted gray with neat white trim. It didn't look like a boarding house, but I couldn't be certain. Pearl opened the front door and led Rider inside. The door shut and I let out the breath I had been holding.

I walked past the house, pretending I had urgent business at the end of the block. I could see that the back yard was enclosed by a low picket fence, and that tall, neatly trimmed shrubs separated the house from its neighbors. White curtains hung in all the windows. I circled the block. Behind the house, someone's vegetable garden covered an entire vacant lot.

I stopped and looked around. No one was in sight. I darted into the garden, heading toward rows of tall pole beans where I could hide.

The yard inside the picket fence was shaded with two immense trees that blocked out my view of the windows. What was happening inside? Was Pearl putting Rider down for a nap? The afternoon was insufferably hot. Surely she'd open a bedroom window for him. If I knew which one, perhaps I could reach it. The trees were close enough to the house to offer many opportunities.

Patience, I told myself. If everything else fails, she'll go back for the evening service and probably take Rider with her. As soon as they leave, I'll grab Rider and run. Yes, I can do that.

No, it's all falling apart. I'm too scared, too stupid. I need Grandpa and Hank to help me.

The back door opened. In the doorway, I saw Pearl and Rider. She'd changed his clothes. He was wearing blue pants and a white shirt, and carrying a toy truck.

Pearl helped him down the steps, stooped, and said something. He nodded and walked across the grass toward a picnic table that sat near the back fence. Pearl watched him for a moment, then turned and went back in the house. She shut the door, but it didn't latch, and so she shut it again, harder. Rider looked back at the house when he heard the sound. Then, silently, sadly, he continued on toward the table.

I waited with my hands pressed against my mouth. Rider sat on the grass next to the table and turned the truck upside down, spinning the wheels the way he'd always done with his toy trucks and cars. I saw his chest rise and fall with a sigh.

I crept out from the rows of pole beans and inched my way toward the fence. Was he near enough to the pickets so that I could reach him? I wasn't certain.

Would he recognize me? What if he didn't? What if he cried out for Pearl?

When I reached the fence, I stood up and tried to speak his name, but I couldn't make a sound.

He must have heard my heart beating. He looked straight at me, then scrambled to his feet and ran toward me, holding up his arms.

"Pick me up, sis," he said. His gray eyes were luminous and his lower lip trembled.

I reached for him and he wrapped his arms around my neck, nearly strangling me. "We're going home," I told him.

But Pearl Sweet had seen me and she came screaming out the back door, running, stumbling, running again, her hands like claws.

✵ Sixteen

I clutched Rider to my chest and backed away from the fence, nearly tripping on the soft earth.

"Give me that child!" Pearl shouted. She had reached the fence and she stretched over it, arms out, her face contorted.

Rider buried his face in my neck. I felt him trembling.

"Rider is my brother," I said. I backed up another step. "I'm Rachel Chance, and you know he's my brother. I'm taking him home to our mother now."

"He's Jim, Junior, and you're not taking him anywhere. Give him to me right now or I'll go in the house to call the police."

"Call them," I said. "I'll tell them how your husband and Pastor Woodie set fire to our pasture and stole my brother while Grandpa and I were saving the cows."

She blinked, and for a moment I thought she was going to give up. But then she lunged over the fence, almost falling on it. "Give him back to me. Jimmy! Jim, Junior! You tell her who you are!"

Rider didn't answer. His little hands clutched my hair

so hard that tears were forming in my eyes. I remembered Druid Annie telling me about her dream, where Rider had been renamed after Pearl's dead child, and I knew with cold certainty that Annie had dreamed true. Suddenly I thought of what to say next that would hurt and frighten her.

"Don't you ever wonder what your dead boy thinks about your giving my brother his name?" I asked. "Do you suppose your little dead baby knows that you don't love him anymore? That you want to forget about him? Now that you're a sinner, you won't go to heaven and he'll never see you again. Do you think he knows that yet? Do you think he's afraid?"

She didn't move or speak at first, but only stared at Rider. "I'll call the police," she said finally. "If you take him, they'll bring him right back."

"I've got his handprint," I said. "I can prove he's ours and that you stole him."

She licked her dry lips. "You're lying."

"No. There are other people with me, coming right behind me, people who know everything you did. You and your brother will go to jail. Everybody, everywhere, will know what you did."

After a long time, she sighed, and her arms dropped to her sides.

"Get out of here," she said. And she turned and walked back to the house.

I ran with Rider out of the garden and down the street, and I kept running, without regard to where I was going. If we were lost, then no one could find us, not Pearl, if she changed her mind, not Billy Bong, not the men in the black suits. Not even the police. I hadn't been as certain as I'd tried to sound that the police would be impressed with my story. I couldn't trust anyone.

By luck, not intent, I found that we were on the right side of town. The road to Ellensburg couldn't be far away. But there were long, dangerous hours until dark, and I was still afraid of Pearl. I had to hide Rider somewhere. And he was hungry and fretful.

In a small grocery store, I used some of my precious money to buy Rider ice cream in a cardboard tub, a small bottle of milk, and two pears. The woman who waited on me stared curiously at us, and I hoped that she didn't notice my shaking hands.

"You must be visiting around here," she said as she put the bottle in a paper sack.

"Yes," I said.

She added the pears to the sack. "I didn't think I'd seen you before. Who are you staying with?"

My mouth was so dry that I had trouble speaking. "The Smiths," I mumbled.

"There's nobody around here named Smith," she declared.

"Ice cream!" Rider demanded, reaching for the small cardboard tub.

The woman laughed. "He knows what's good on a hot day. Is he your brother?"

"No," I blurted. "He's my nephew. Sammy Peterson, from Portland, Oregon." I reached for the sack.

She pushed it toward me. "Well, you enjoy your stay. But I can't for the life of me think of a Smith family in this neighborhood."

"We've been on a long walk and I just remembered that I was supposed to bring home milk," I said. I took Rider's hand and led him toward the door.

I was so nervous my ears were ringing. What if someone began searching for us and came here? Would the woman remember that I'd said Rider was my nephew Sammy from Portland and not bother mentioning us? No. She'd remember that I'd said we were visiting the Smith family and there was no Smith family in this neighborhood.

Quickly, I turned off that street onto a narrow road barely wide enough for one car. The houses here were small and shabby, and the yards looked scorched. A dog barked at us from one porch, and a woman came out and took him inside, slamming the door behind her.

"Ice cream!" Rider demanded again. His treat was melting in the sack.

As soon as we turned the corner, I sat him down and gave him the ice cream, helping him spoon it into his mouth and wiping his mouth with his shirttail. No one watched us.

When he was finished, I carried him into the overgrown yard by a house that looked empty, and we sat in the dry grass on the shady side and ate the rest of our meal. Rider fell asleep holding half a pear in one hand. His other hand clutched a fold of my skirt tightly.

I didn't mean to sleep but I did, and when I woke, the western sky was blazing. Hank had told me to be on the road to Ellensburg at dark, when it was safer for Rider and me to walk. But I knew I'd better find the road before it was too dark to read road signs, and so I woke Rider, and we left our quiet sanctuary.

Most people seemed to be indoors, eating dinner. Through open windows, I heard voices as we passed houses close to the street. Sometimes I heard radios. Occasionally a car would pass us, but no one paid attention to us. Still, I was frightened and Rider caught my fright and whimpered as I carried him.

"Wanna go home," he said.

"That's where we're going," I told him. "Mama's waiting, and Jonah, too. And Banjo."

"Where's Gimpa?" he said. "I want Gimpa."

"Grandpa's coming in the truck," I said, hoping that what I said was true. "Grandpa and Hank, and Annie, too."

"Put me down."

I was glad he wanted to walk for a while, because my arms ached. A block farther along, I found the highway to Ellensburg. It was still too light for us to be on that road, and so I told Rider that we were going to rest for a bit and I led him to a crooked pine tree where the low branches would shelter us until dark. I could watch and not be seen. Even though Hank hadn't planned on being here this soon, I was afraid to take any chances. If the truck came along early, I'd be able to run out and stop it. If it came. If Hank had been able to fix it. But I didn't dare dwell on that. I was scared enough.

The clear evening light lingered, fading gently into early twilight. Rider dozed next to me, his breathing quiet. Cars passed, some disappearing down the highway to Ellensburg, others turning off on a dusty road across from us.

Another car approached, but this one stopped. A man got out, waved, and the car turned down the dirt road, raising a cloud of chalky dust.

The man watched it, then shouldered a blanket roll and pushed his hat to the back of his head. He looked behind, down the road from Yakima, then ahead toward Ellensburg and the mountain pass.

And then he looked at us. He was Rider's father.

I scrambled to my feet. "Where are you going?" I shouted to him. "Wait. Please! Don't leave us here."

He shook his head as if he didn't believe what he was seeing. "Rachel? Rachel!" He dropped his blanket roll and started toward me, holding out his arms. "My God, girl, I looked everywhere for you. You scared me to death."

He threw his arms around me and hugged me until I thought my ribs would crack. "Casey drove the bus up and down every street near where I saw you, but you were gone. So I decided that I'd better go to Lara and find out what was going on. What are you doing so far from home?"

"I came to get Rider," I said. "He was stolen." I was so stunned at finding him that for a moment I forgot that he didn't know who Rider was. "Rider's my brother," I added. "He's sleeping now."

But he wasn't. Rider stood behind me, his thumb in his mouth.

"His hair's the wrong color," I blurted. Stupidly, I began crying. "The people who stole him dyed it. They changed his name, too. He's not Jim, Junior. He's Rider, and he's really blond, like Mama. Like you." I wiped my tears away with the back of my hand and bit my lip hard. What would he do? Would he be angry?

The man's astonished expression froze. He bent down and studied Rider for a long time, as if my brother were a book that he had longed to read. Finally he said softly, "I'll take you back to your mother, Rachel. Don't worry anymore. Everything's going to be all right after this." He picked up his son.

"What's your name?" I asked him. "What do we call you?"

He looked down into Rider's puzzled face. "Why, you'd both better call me dad," he said, and then he threw back his head and laughed.

So we walked and talked on the road toward home. I told him how Rider came to be stolen from us, and how Grandpa, Annie, Hank, and I set out to steal him back. I told him that Betty-Dean was dying in our barn, and that the cousins had lost their farm. And I told him about Mama and Jonah, who had been, in their own sad ways, almost as lost to us as Rider.

Stars flared above us in the night sky. A warm wind blew my skirt and ruffled my hair. Rider slept on his father's shoulder.

The gray-eyed man told me about crop chasing with Casey Shay and his men. "After we finished our work in Spokane, we intended going to California," he said. "If you'd come to Eastern Washington one week later, I'd have been gone."

"I couldn't have come later," I said. "Billy Bong's leaving Eastern Washington, too. We had to be here now."

He glanced down at me and even though it was dark, I knew he was smiling. "And you were prepared to walk all the way to Ellensburg?"

"In the morning I'd have flagged down a bus if one came

along," I said. "If I'd had to, that is. But Hank promised that he'd find me, and I'm trying hard to believe that he can."

We stopped talking and walked in a warm, companionable silence. I wasn't afraid anymore. I wasn't even tired.

After a while, we heard a fearful racket behind us. I knew before I looked that Hank had performed another miracle on his enemy, the truck.

I waved Hank to a stop. To my astonishment, he leaped out of the truck, leaving the engine running. "Who's that man?" he shouted. "What's he doing with Rider?"

I grabbed him before he grabbed Rider's father. "It's Rider's dad!" I cried. "Honestly! It's really him."

Hank drew a deep breath. "Are you all right, Rachel? How long have you been walking? Did you have any trouble?"

"Everything was fine. I'll tell you later." Grandpa was struggling to his feet in the back of the truck, and I jumped up beside him. "I've got Rider, Grandpa. He remembered me and he's been asking for you. And I found his father — "

"I heard," Grandpa grumbled. "Everybody can hear you, clear to Spokane." He held out his arms, and Rider's father put his sleeping son into them. Grandpa bent his head over Rider and kissed his forehead.

Then he looked sharply at me. "Judas H. Priest," he growled, "if you aren't a sight to strike a man blind, Rachel. When was the last time you combed your hair?"

Druid Annie reached over the side of the truck bed to pat Rider, and then said to me, "Did I see true?"

"Yes." A sudden fright shook me when I remembered Pearl at the fence, her claws reaching.

"Now just listen to them!" Grandpa grumbled. "If it's not poultices, it's tea leaves and spooky dreams. Let's get going before the truck stops again and I kick its slats in and leave it for dead right in the middle of the highway." He gestured at Rider's father. "You, sir, hop right up here beside me. You've got some explaining to do."

Hank helped Annie back in the truck and got behind the wheel again. I leaned against Grandpa and fell asleep as the men talked. We were going home.

Hank left us at Ellensburg and turned east once more, to complete his interrupted journey. We wouldn't see him again for five years, when the Second World War ended. Then he came home for me.

*

"You didn't tell everything about our trip," Hank said when he finished reading this manuscript.

"Didn't I? Are you sure?" I asked, concerned as I shuffled through the pages.

He put his hand on my shoulder. "You forgot to tell them that you let me kiss you goodbye that night you ran off to get Rider by yourself."

I laughed. "This story isn't about us."

"Rachel," Hank said, "every story is about us."

AVON FLARE BESTSELLERS

by BRUCE AND CAROLE HART

STRUT   75962-4/$3.99US/$4.99Can
She's not going to stop till she rocks to the top.

NOW OR NEVER   75963-2/$3.50US/$4.25Can
Michael Skye, the rock star who broke Jessie's heart,
is back in town. And back in her life—if she lets him.

WAITING GAMES   79012-2/$3.50US/$4.25Can
Michael and Jessie's story continues as they learn
what being in love really means. How much are they
willing to share together—if their love is to last forever?

SOONER OR LATER   42978-0/$2.95US/$3.50Can

BREAKING UP IS HARD TO DO
                          89970-1/$3.50US/$3.95Can

CROSS YOUR HEART 89971-X/$3.50US/$4.25Can

NOVELS FROM AVON FLARE

CLASS PICTURES	61408-1/$2.95 US/$3.50 Can

Marilyn Sachs

Pat, always the popular one, and shy, plump Lolly have been best friends since kindergarten, through thick and thin, supporting each other during crises. But everything changes when Lolly turns into a thin, pretty blonde and Pat finds herself playing second fiddle for the first time.

BABY SISTER	70358-1/$3.50 US/$4.25 Can

Marilyn Sachs

Her sister was everything Penny could never be, until Penny found something else.

THE GROUNDING OF GROUP 6	83386-7/$3.99 US/$4.99 Can

Julian Thompson

What do parents do when they realize that their sixteen-year old son or daughter is a loser and an embarrassment to the family? Five misfits find they've been set up to disappear at exclusive Coldbrook School, but aren't about to allow themselves to be permanently "grounded."

TAKING TERRI MUELLER	79004-1/$3.50 US/$4.25 Can

Norma Fox Mazer

Was it possible to be kidnapped by your own father? Terri's father has always told her that her mother died in a car crash—but now Terri has reason to suspect differently, and she struggles to find the truth on her own.

WHEN DOES THE FUN START?	76129-7/$3.50 US/$4.25 Can

Jean Thesman

Nothing has been any fun for Teddy Gideon since she spotted Zack, the love of her life, gazing into the eyes of another girl—a beautiful girl Teddy has never seen before.

AVON FLARE ◆ NOVELS
FROM BESTSELLING AUTHOR
MARILYN SACHS